G R JORDAN

A Personal Favour

A Kirsten Stewart Thriller

First edition

ISBN: 978-1-915562-20-3

This book was professionally typeset on Reedsy. Find out more at reedsy.com

I like these cold, grey winter days.
Days like these let you savour a bad
mood.

BILL WATTERSON

Contents

Foreword

The events of this book, while based in a region of Alaska, are in an entirely fictional setting and all persons are entirely fictitious. Kyler's Peak is a fictitious town based on no Alaskan settlement.

Acknowledgement

To Ken, Jean, Colin, Evelyn, John and Rosemary for your work in bringing this novel to completion, your time and effort is deeply appreciated.

Novels by G R Jordan

The Highlands and Islands Detective series (Crime)

1. Water's Edge
2. The Bothy
3. The Horror Weekend
4. The Small Ferry
5. Dead at Third Man
6. The Pirate Club
7. A Personal Agenda
8. A Just Punishment
9. The Numerous Deaths of Santa Claus
10. Our Gated Community
11. The Satchel
12. Culhwch Alpha
13. Fair Market Value
14. The Coach Bomber
15. The Culling at Singing Sands
16. Where Justice Fails
17. The Cortado Club
18. Cleared to Die
19. Man Overboard!
20. Antisocial Behaviour
21. Rogues' Gallery
22. The Death of Macleod - Inferno Book 1

The Patrick Smythe Series (Crime)

1. The Disappearance of Russell Hadleigh
2. The Graves of Calgary Bay
3. The Fairy Pools Gathering

Austerley & Kirkgordon Series (Fantasy)

1. Crescendo!
2. The Darkness at Dillingham
3. Dagon's Revenge
4. Ship of Doom

Supernatural and Elder Threat Assessment Agency (SETAA)
Series (Fantasy)

1. Scarlett O'Meara: Beastmaster

Island Adventures Series (Cosy Fantasy Adventure)

1. Surface Tensions

Dark Wen Series (Horror Fantasy)

1. The Blasphemous Welcome
2. The Demon's Chalice

Chapter 01

Melissa stomped her feet on the snowy ground, her coat pulled tight around her. She watched as the snowflakes danced, twirling in the night breeze, spinning here and there before landing on her coat. They would eventually melt, taken by the heat of her own body from within the coat, but outside of her, the snow was falling thickly everywhere. She stood beside the bridge looking down at the river, hearing it rush along. On the far side was a single lamp, and the shadows were pushed back, but not as far as herself. It was a clandestine meeting after all. She needed to stay unobserved, away from others.

There had been footprints here when she'd first arrived, and she wondered if they were from her contact. After all, if you'd arranged to meet someone, would you not have got there first, checked out the land to make sure nobody else was there? The issue was sensitive. It involved many of the town's senior figures, or at least it looked that way. She couldn't be sure. There was no concrete evidence. But this woman? She would know. She would be able to say.

Her boss at the paper didn't believe her. Melissa could sense that. Martin was nice enough, but he was an old hack. An

American through and through, he'd been a part of Kyler's Peak all his life. While he wasn't exactly well respected, he was loved in the same way that fixtures around your house are loved. Sure, if they break, you might throw them out, but it reminded you of where you were from the time that they existed.

Melissa turned and looked back at the bridge. How had she ended up here? She had dreams when she'd started of joining a newspaper back in England. Having grown up in Birmingham, she had traded in the concrete jungle for the wilds of Alaska, and Kyler's Peak was certainly out there. It was a *nothing* town in some ways, on the way to other places, with maybe some fifteen thousand of a population. Big enough to have things, but small enough to be unimportant to anywhere else.

Still, they'd given her a chance to be a senior reporter for whatever that was worth. She had never expected it—never expected to come across a story that if true was a scandal that linked to other parts of America. Other parts that scared her. She was unsure now what to do. Martin had been of no use. 'Just get me evidence,' he'd said. 'It's not a story without evidence. We can't run with speculation.' Then his last words, something he had never said. 'Be careful.' That was when she knew she was onto something. Martin must have seen it, must have had an inkling about it. He never told her to take care. It was Kyler's Peak after all.

When the restaurant had rats running through it and she'd gone to interview the owner, he never told her to be careful. Yet the owner was a raging hotbed, claiming people had put the rats there. He might have been right as well, for the rival restaurant across town had seen a lift in business. When she'd done that truck-stop piece about the extra upload of semis

2

coming through, as they called them here. 'Articulated lorries,' they would have said back home. Somebody had tried to warn her off about mentioning it, but Martin had never said, 'Be careful.' Now, she felt there was danger, a danger that she didn't fully understand.

A contact worked in the mayor's office. She knew the bids that had gone in; this person would have seen them. A low-level clerk, but one of those minor people in life who gets to see the important documents. They never heard the conversations that were too important to be written down, but they saw other things. Kyler's Peak was famous, or at least a place of historical importance because of the gold in the area. It had been mined over a hundred and fifty years ago in great rushes, but now standing here, Melissa found it hard to believe.

The mining was long gone, but someone had said there was an old mine for sale. Claims had been made by local people to it and a bidding process was offered, the land currently owned by the local area. Envelopes would be entered with sealed bids. There would have been a bit of friction because some of those bids had come from people from out of town. That was one thing she learned about Kyler's Peak. It was local. They were wary of anyone from the outside.

She had suffered it on arrival, but she had known how to play them, or the men at least, being nineteen years of age, with long blonde hair, and a reasonable figure. At least she believed so, still basking in the confidence of youth. She used her womanly charm to disarm the men, pushed past their scepticism of this person who had come into their community. She had also written some decent pieces in the paper, which had been well received. That helped. But the women were always watchful of her because she wasn't one of them. Martin was. That's why he was tolerated, because in truth, Melissa believed she wrote a lot better than he.

Melissa stamped her feet again. *Was the contact not coming? She could have said.* It was bloody freezing, even for here. She was about to turn away when she heard a noise from downstream. It was almost like a yell or scream that had started but wasn't allowed to finish. Inside Melissa, the fire of journalism roared. Where most people would run from a scream, worried for their safety, Melissa leapt towards it, looking for the story.

She tore off down the banks, aware that the wind around her would mask most of the sound she was making as she stomped through the snow. The sound of the river would add to it. She was fairly confident that she could arrive on the scene without being heard. Inside, her heart pounded. Here, thousands of miles from where she'd grown up, in a land that wasn't hers, she was chasing down a story again. Was it connected to her contact?

The contact had given the name Alice and no other details. When Melissa had checked the mayor's office, they employed no one called Alice. Maybe she'd see her face and recognise her because she had checked through photographs of the staff she could find. They ranged from those about to retire down to girls as young as herself. When the voice had spoken to her on the phone in the paper's office, she reckoned it was disguised, maybe coming through a handkerchief or one of those voice boxes. Nowadays, you could do so much so easily.

Another half-hearted scream and then a thump. She couldn't be far away now. Melissa ducked past some trees and came across a scene beside the river.

There were three men standing there and she recognised

4

none of them. That being said, they had scars across their faces, large parka coats on, but she saw tailored trousers and black leather shoes. Clearly three people that weren't used to being out here in the wild. She had her own snow boots on. In fact, anybody from the town would do that. It was the time of year for them, a time of year when you didn't venture out without a warm coat, gloves, hat, and thick boots.

The three men formed a small circle around a woman on her knees. She looked middle-aged and tears were streaming down her face. One of the men was holding her by the hair and using it, he yanked her head back, exposing her neck. His colleague was standing in front of the woman and delivered several blows to her face with the back of his hand. She seemed to be getting beyond the point of screaming, now just suffering. Melissa watched as blood trickled out of her mouth. The woman's coat had been pulled back, her arms were now trapped behind her, but there was nothing sexual about what was occurring. This seemed to be a beating, good and proper.

Melissa crouched down in the snow, trying not to gasp at what she was looking at. She's seen people getting beaten before, had been around fights, but these men looked serious, intent on causing the woman grief. More than that, there was a third one. He just stood and stared at them. He was silent in an eerie way, and when Melissa saw the man delivering the beatings look over at him, she realised that this silent man was the boss.

A switchblade was taken out and held up to the woman's throat while the man whispered something in her ear. She shook her head.

'I don't know. God's sake, I don't know.'

The man in front of her looked over at his boss, who simply

gave a nod. The switchblade was taken across her neck and the man stepped out of the way as blood began to spurt. Melissa could hear her desperately choking, trying to catch her breath, she tumbled to the ground, hands racing to her neck. Melissa staggered backwards from her crouched position, went to turn to run, and fell over a small post beside the river. She caused it to topple and her hand reached out desperately as it slid down the bank before hitting the water and causing a splash.

She glanced back in a panic towards the men and saw their heads flick round, looking directly at her. *Hell!* she thought. *Hell! Run!*

She spun onto her front, pushed herself up and started to take off through the trees. She put her hands in front of her, knocking branches out of the way, for she could hear them behind her. There was a blind panic forming inside her, but she tried to focus, tried to find the gaps between the trees, not to simply run into any large branches that would knock her to the ground. She ducked this way and that, then felt a branch scrape across her face. She put a gloved hand out and when she looked back down at it, she swore there was blood on it, but Melissa didn't stop. They were still behind; they were still coming, for she could hear their panting.

She'd reached the bridge she'd been at earlier, ran into the light racing across it, but by the time she'd made it halfway across she could hear them, their footsteps approaching. She jumped off the end of the bridge into deeper snow. She hadn't intended to, as she had thought the path should swing harder to the right, but it wasn't there, and she sank down to her knees quickly. She tried to pump her legs, tried to keep going. A quick glance back and she saw the men jump into the snow behind her. They too sank deeply. Melissa reached with her hands to the left, pushing down with them and forcing herself out of the deeper snow back onto the path.

As she went to run again, she felt a hand clip her foot which in turn caught her other foot, tripping her up and sending her sprawling on the snowy path. She screamed. She was in the middle of nowhere, out alone in the dark of the night. The three men after her had cut the throat of the woman. What chance did she have? She flipped over onto her backside and saw the men dragging themselves out of the deep snow back onto the path. She rolled over, picked herself up, began to run and slipped on an icy part of the path. She slid forward but didn't get her hands up in time as she connected with a tree and fell back down hard on the path.

Her head cracked off the solid ice below and she slid round, coming to a halt at the edge of the path. Groggily, she tried to find purchase, to be able to move again and she saw one of the men coming towards her. His leather shoes betrayed him, for he slipped on the ice and fell hard on his backside. In another time and place it would have seemed comical, but she didn't laugh, too aware there were two more following him as the next came towards her. She tried to push with her feet and slid back slightly along the path, but she was going nowhere fast. A hand came down, picked her up by the blouse she was wearing underneath her coat. He was strong and held her up to level with him.

'No idea, boss,' said the man behind him. 'Could be anybody.'

The last thing Melissa thought was *how did people not know her? Everybody knew who she was in the town. She'd only been here six months, but she was that young reporter girl. How did they not know her?* She never got to form a conclusion for a fist hit her hard around the temple and the world went dark.

Chapter 02

Kirsten Stewart cut open the fresh packet of coffee beans and dipped her nose into it. It was a housewarming gift from her former boss, Detective Inspector Seoras Macleod, and she noted it was the brand he always liked. Seoras had been fussy about coffee when she'd been there. Every time they met, he still was, but Kirsten loved the thought rather than the coffee. She took the beans, poured them into a separate container before taking a handful and grinding them up. Once she'd sorted the filter coffee machine, she switched it on and turned, leaning back against the kitchen worktop, looking around the flat she was in.

The world had changed greatly from her days working with Macleod. In recent times, it had changed beyond all recognition. She'd found the love of her life and she'd taken Craig away to a Greek island looking for time alone together. Their previous life in the secret services had caught up with them and now Craig was left maimed. He'd lost both legs below the knees.

Having come back to the UK, they'd once again taken up residence in Inverness, this time in a specially adapted flat. She'd made sure all the mods cons were there, all the devices to help Craig get about the house to be as independent as possible. She tried to make things as before. But she couldn't: he was wheelchair-bound now.

At first, he'd refused to let her push him saying he needed to learn himself, but that would take time. While he was determined, she saw his frustration and the frustration turned to anger if she sought to step in and help. There were times when she'd sit endlessly waiting for him to build up strength to push himself on. All he had to do was let her push him, take him around places. After all, they were still together, still a partnership, still a team, and hopefully one day, lovers again.

Kirsten heard the gurgle of the coffee, estimated there must be enough in there for a cup, and turning, made herself one. She could hear the shower still running and so resumed her position, looking around the open flat in front of her. It was on the ground floor but had plenty of security features as well. Just because Craig was maimed didn't mean that their old life would go away completely. Kirsten was always on the lookout.

They now had the worry of bills for although they had put a little aside, she would need to return to work of some sort. She reckoned they had maybe another three or four months before finances would start to become tight. There was no disability payoff from the service, for Craig had left it along with her. No one would admit to the incident out in Zante that had caused these troubles. There was that horrific moment that she replayed in her mind, on the point of losing him to the Russians, and then watching the missile that took out the boat he was on.

Kirsten adjusted her dressing gown, feeling a little cold and wanting to get into the shower. In the old days, she wouldn't have hesitated. She'd have walked in, stripped off and joined

Craig. That was something that happened several times a week in those heady days when they were just enjoying each other, finding their love. She'd tried to walk in the other day, but he told her to get out. Even lovemaking, if you could call it that, had changed, for all he seemed to be able to do was lie there, like her personal mannequin. Whether that would change in the future, who knew?

Maybe when he regained his strength he would be able to not seem like a patient, but it was getting to her. The fact the intimacy had been lost, that he wouldn't allow her to be that way with him while not allowing her to help him. She understood that to a degree; he'd always been an independent person. When you worked for the service, you were taught that. You learned how to look after yourself, but nothing prepared you for something like this.

There was a thud from the shower and a yell, and Kirsten sat down the coffee and ran through to the shower room. Opening the door, she saw Craig on the floor of the shower, struggling to raise himself back up onto the little seat that he occupied when showering.

'Get out; I'm fine,' he said.

'Are you sure?' asked Kirsten. 'I can give you a hand.'

'No, I'm fine. I'm bloody fine. Just leave me be.'

'It's not helping. It's okay. I can help you. This is us. This isn't the world outside. This is you and me. We have to help each other.'

'What help do you need?' he spat. 'Was it you that got kidnapped? Was it you that got taken away? No. You had to come and save me. Look at me. I can't do bloody anything.'

He threw a fist at the shower door hitting it with such force that Kirsten was worried he might crack it.

'You can beat the hell out of that if you want. Doesn't make any difference. Why don't you let me come in with you? Let me shower you. We used to do that. Remember?'

She'd hoped that the memory might have spawned a happier face, but instead, she could see the bitterness. He waved the hand at her, motioning for her to get out, and she turned away, feeling the tears rolling down her face. She wouldn't do that to him. She wouldn't cry in front of him, for he was suffering enough.

Closing the shower door behind her, she walked back to take up her coffee again. Would they ever be the same again? Was there any way in which Craig could be the same? He'd been such a gentleman, such a considerate person. Now, there was something in him that she really didn't like. He would take no pity from her, which was understandable for there was a pride in him, but she'd expected that he would've coped better.

Underneath, Kirsten was a fighter brought up in the mixed martial arts ring where you just kept going until they hit you with that punch that puts you down for the count. She saw Craig's condition as the same thing, but he didn't and she didn't understand why she couldn't see his side. He wouldn't tell her his view, his trouble. He just banished her from his life for now. Even at night in the bed, he wouldn't accept her cuddling.

The telephone ringing snapped her from her thoughts, and she strolled over, picking it up and walking to the window of the flat.

'You're through to Craig and Kirsten's,' she said, trying to sound cheery but knowing she'd failed.

'I need to speak to Craig. He's an old friend.'

'He's currently in the shower; this is Kirsten. You can tell me.'

'No, I can't. I need to speak to Craig specifically.'

'Can I ask who's calling then?' asked Kirsten.

'No, no, best I just speak to Craig. He'll know what to do.'

Kirsten bit her lip not wanting to tell the person on the other end of the phone that Craig can barely shower himself at the moment, never mind work out anybody else's problems. Instead, she turned and knocked the door of the shower room. On opening it, she found him back up in his seat, washing down.

'Call for you. Won't speak to me—said they have to speak to you. No name.'

She saw Craig's eyes narrow, and he turned around, switching off the shower. She went to get him a towel, but he told her to leave it and she watched as using his hands, he dragged himself through and picked the towel off the rail. He was unbalanced as he dragged himself, sitting on his bottom. At one point he toppled. Once again, he refused help and once he had a towel wrapped round him, he took the phone off her, almost dismissing her out of the room.

Back in the main living area of the flat, Kirsten walked to the window again and stared out at the Inverness street across from her. She used to like a high-up flat. You could see really well, whereas here you just saw across the road. You also had to be more careful now with how you walked around the flat for the windows were copious and large, letting in large amounts of light, but also giving a view from the street for anyone walking past.

If they had been intimate, Kirsten would be worried that she'd leave curtains open. That'd been her habit when she lived up in higher flats, not having to worry about anyone peeking in. She realised the train of thought was just trying

12

to block out the way Craig was and the call he was having. If it was somebody in trouble, he wouldn't be able to help. He'd feel more useless; of that, she was sure. It was twenty minutes before the shower room door opened and she watched him haul himself up into his chair and begin to wheel himself round towards the sofa. He'd managed to put on a pair of pants and a t-shirt.

'Who was that?'

'Old friend. His daughter's out in Alaska and she's gone missing; wants me to go out there.'

'And?'

'Well, I can hardly go, can I?' he barked.

'No, you can't at the moment,' said Kirsten. 'Your head's not clear for one.'

He snorted. 'Of course, it's not bloody clear. What can I do for him, eh?'

'You could go and check it out,' said Kirsten. 'You could go and find out what was happening. You've got a brain.'

'How can I damn well go?' asked Craig. 'Can barely operate around this bloody flat.' She watched as the phone sailed out of his hand, missing her by about two feet and smashing on the far wall. 'Told him you'd have to go.'

Kirsten looked at Craig. 'Me? How can I go? You need me. You need me here. You need me.'

'Because I'm some sort of invalid? Because I'm some sort of . . .'

'Because you need help,' said Kirsten. 'You need somebody to walk you through this.'

'That's going to be you?' he said. 'You're going to walk me through this?'

'You know I will. I'm here for the long haul, Craig. I'm here beside you.'

'I don't bloody well want you beside me; do you not get that?'

Kirsten felt tears coming through her eyes and her hands were beginning to shake. *What was he saying?*

'What do you mean?' she asked.

'Every time I look at you, do you know what I see? I don't see a partner. I see someone who reminds me of what I used to be.'

'We were always more than that. We weren't just two agents; we were more.'

'Maybe we were,' he said. 'Now, I'm just the invalid. I'm just the guy who can't do things. You're the one who's going to have to go out and get a job and feed me. I still struggle to reach that cooker properly. Still struggle to do anything. I struggle to have a dump in the toilet.'

'I still want you. I want you. I want the Craig who's in there, the one I used to know.'

'You think he's coming back? You think I'm just going to be the way I was? Look at me. Look at me. The state of me. You need to go. He needs help and I can't give it.'

'No,' said Kirsten, 'people can take care of their own problems. We've got our problem.'

'Yes, I'm a problem now, aren't I? I'm not an adventure. I'm not a wild party. I'm just somebody that needs taking care of.'

'I will take care of you,' said Kirsten. 'Whatever it takes.'

'No, you won't,' said Craig suddenly. 'I need space. I need bloody space now. I can't have you all over me. Every time I look at you, I hate what I am. Do you understand that?'

Kirsten didn't and the tears streamed down her face.

'I need space. I need space to deal with me, so you are going to bloody Alaska. You're going to go and help my friend find his daughter.'

Chapter 03

Kirsten stepped off the bus at Inverness Airport and looked at the metal-sheet-clad terminal as the rain bounced off it. She was going to travel light to Alaska and buy some clothing on arrival. She'd checked the internet and it would be cold, and she reckoned they would have the best gear for it. She was in her boots, black jeans, black T-shirt and leather jacket, feeling as comfortable as she could but inside, she was falling apart. Craig hadn't even hugged her when she'd left and behind the eyes that only a few months ago would have shone for her, there was a near hatred of who she was. Now she was going to have to be that very person to help Craig's friend.

She had called Mr. Carson, Melissa's father, and had spoken with him in some detail on the phone. His daughter, only nineteen, had gone out to Alaska to work with a newspaper, an opportunity to gain experience, find stories, but she hadn't spoken to him now in over a week. The editor had called, telling him that she'd gone missing and something in his voice had bothered the man. His daughter had said she was onto a story, one that involved outsiders and possibly might have been dangerous. That was the last time they'd spoken—the very night she had vanished.

Kirsten had no idea where she'd gone, but she was living in Kyler's Peak, a place Kirsten didn't know. The map showed it to be on the way to everywhere. Although the town wasn't large, Melissa had been a Birmingham girl, bright, intelligent, and from all that her father was saying, smelt trouble. The man had no sway with the US authorities, but he'd been a friend of Craig's and knew the position that Craig had held before he'd left the service. Unfortunately, he hadn't heard what had happened to Craig, but he was most grateful when Kirsten said she would go. Before she got on the bus, however, Kirsten had phoned a friend asking him to meet her at the airport.

The terminal wasn't a large one, and Kirsten had no problems identifying her friend, sitting with a coffee behind a table in the cafe area. As she approached, she could see the worry on his face.

'It's been a while,' said Seoras Macleod, standing up in his white shirt and tie, his coat lying over his chair. Kirsten leaned forward as he embraced her, holding her tight, but when he went to break off, she held onto him.

'Seoras,' she said. 'He's gone.' Then she cried, clinging onto Macleod, crying.

In his time as her boss, Macleod had never been a touchy-feely character. He was strong, determined, possibly a little arrogant, but right now he didn't flinch, letting her cry her eyes out before she broke off and sat down.

'I see things are not good,' he said. 'Can I make them worse with a rather terrible cup of coffee from this establishment?'

Kirsten gave a small laugh. 'Yes, you can,' she said. 'Are you suffering another one?'

'I'll join you for one but it's just for you. Personally, if they

17

came in here and finished off whoever does this coffee, I wouldn't be unsympathetic towards the killer.'

She watched as he strode over to the counter. He was so particular about his coffee. The stuff probably wasn't that bad, just wasn't what he wanted. There seemed to be an ability to forgive anything except bad coffee. When Macleod returned apologising and placing a cup of coffee in front of her, she watched as he didn't sit back in the chair, but leaned forward, elbows on the table, studying her.

'What's wrong?' he said.

'Craig's missing half his legs. That's what's wrong.'

'He's been missing them for a while now. Thought you had the new flat. You were settling in. It's not his legs, is it?'

'It is his legs. He doesn't feel like a proper person anymore. He doesn't feel like an agent.'

'He's not an agent. Neither are you. You're both out of that, aren't you? Although you seem to be rushing off somewhere, leaving behind a man that you're telling me isn't right.'

'I forgot I was sitting in front of a detective,' she said sharply.

'I don't need to be a detective to work that out. You called me before running off on a plane. If you're calling me, you need help. You wouldn't have called me to cry on my shoulder, even if you wanted to. You wouldn't have thought I would let you.'

'I need a favour,' said Kirsten. 'I need you to look in on Craig; his mind's dark at the moment, very dark. He's struggling and he wants me out of the way.'

'Out of the way?' asked Macleod. 'Why?'

'Because, well, he says he looks at me . . .'

'And he sees everything that he used to be.'

'Exactly,' said Kirsten. 'Exactly. What am I meant to do?

18

Chop my legs off? This is who I am. He fell in love with this person, with me. He didn't need to be like me back then.'

'No, but you were equals.'

'We're equals now. I need help, too. I need him.'

'He doesn't see that,' said Macleod. 'He may never see that. Something you're going to have to live with. He might come out of it. He might not. The way we picture ourselves is important.'

'I just want to hold him. I just want to . . .'

'Do everything for him? It's not what he needs,' said Macleod. 'You need to understand this is his journey. Sometimes we must walk our own line, despite all the people that we love around us. It doesn't necessarily mean that they get to help us. I guess we ultimately stand alone.'

Kirsten's hand trembled on the table as she thought through the comment. She picked up the coffee cup, trying to steady her hand, and raised it to her lips as if it was the first time she'd ever tried to drink. Once the cup had reached the right place, she drank deeply and then put the cup down quickly.

'Blooming hot,' she said. 'Why do they make it so hot?'

'Because they don't know what they're doing with the coffee here. Told you that.'

'Will you look in on him? He might listen to you.'

'Because I'm not a charge-around secret agent? In fact, physically compared to you, I'm nothing. So, you think he'll respond to me instead?'

'I don't know, Seoras. He's not responding to me, is he? He smashed the phone, threw it across the room when he couldn't go and help his friend.'

'His friend? That's where you're going?'

'Friend's daughter is missing in Alaska.'

19

'Have you contacted the authorities? Do you want me to do that? I can probably get a link through somewhere, find someone.'

'No,' she said. 'The authorities there reckon she probably just skipped town, not coming back. I'm not sure how cooperative they're going to be. I'm not sure if they're involved or not. I'm not sure of anything until I get out there. I'm going in cold and I'm going in quiet. This is reconnaissance until I find out what's going on. If I need you, I'll call you.'

'Very good,' said Macleod. 'In the meantime, I'll check up on him.'

'I went into this secret life,' she said. 'How come I don't trust anyone in it, but I trust you? I would trust Hope. I would trust Ross. Trust the team from the old days without a moment's hesitation, the team I had, but I don't trust my team in the service.'

'It's just a hard time,' said Macleod. 'You need to go somewhere and focus. You need to get away from Craig for a bit, too. You're not neglecting him. You're doing what he wants you to do, and I'll pop in. I'll keep an eye.' The pair sat in silence, Kirsten drinking up her coffee before hearing her flight on the Tannoy.

'I haven't even checked in. I better go and do that. Look, Seoras,' she said standing up, and watching the man stand up to meet her, 'thank you. Thank you as always.'

She put out her hand to shake it, but he stepped forward and hugged her. 'Whatever you need, you know I'm here. Take very good care.'

Kirsten fought to stop herself from crying again and made it to the ticket desk and then through security before she felt a flood of tears overcome her as she sat in departures. It wasn't long to wait, however, before she was boarding a plane, her eyes still foggy and crying. As she mounted the steps up into the plane bound for London Heathrow, she saw another man also boarding . . . and he was staring at her.

It wasn't uncommon in her life that men would stare at Kirsten. She had a good figure, and she was happy at casual glances. If someone continued to stare, yes, it could get creepy and she'd soon dissuade them, but this man was looking in a way that didn't indicate pleasure in viewing her. She felt there was something more sinister behind his eyes as if he were measuring her up.

Maybe she was just feeling off-kilter. Kirsten boarded the plane, took her seat towards the back of it, and drifted off as they ascended above the clouds and flew down to London.

On arrival, Kirsten checked in to an airport hotel, having to stay the night before flying out the next day. She'd be off to Anchorage, and from there, would travel across by car to Kyler's Peak. As she sat in the restaurant that night in the hotel, her dinner of fish and potatoes in front of her, she tried to run through what she knew about the missing girl. In truth, it wasn't a lot, and she was going in empty-handed. There were no weapons coming. She was going in as purely recon.

Maybe she should have taken something to defend herself with, but that would raise eyebrows. Surely, American officials would know who she was, although whether or not they would pull her in would be another matter. That was a thing about the spy community. You didn't show your hand, you didn't show what you understood, and you kept everything secret until you needed to.

The fish had been overdone and dry, the potatoes under-cooked, and the carrots that came along with them were frankly rather disappointing. She thought about taking a book to bed but instead was rather intrigued by a man three tables away. He kept looking up and over at her, and in truth, she was enjoying the attention. Craig had been giving her none these last couple of months. Not that she had any intentions about doing anything about it, but sometimes it was nice to be admired, and she glanced just long enough at the man. He was maybe in his mid-thirties and had an affable smile.

She saw a face pass the window outside the restaurant. It was the face of the man who had watched her board the flight at Inverness, the man who had got on the flight, and he was now wandering around Heathrow. Maybe it was just coincidence. Maybe he was also waiting for a flight in the morning. He wasn't dining near her after all, but then if she was tailing someone, she wouldn't either. Maybe she was paranoid. That was the trouble with the job she did, you got paranoid. You got worried that everybody was after you, nervous about what was going on. Every deft smile, every little action took on a significance that generally was blown out of proportion.

She stood up and made her way over to the lift to take her up to her room. She saw the young man leave his table and join her in the lift. Kirsten stood on one side, he on the other and once the doors are closed, he turned to her.

'Sorry, I couldn't help but stare. I hope I wasn't freaking you out.'

'Not at all,' said Kirsten. 'It's fine.'

'My name is Tom. I'm just down here for a conference.'

'I'm Kirsten,' she said, 'flying out tomorrow.'

'I don't suppose you want to get a drink at the bar,' he said. 'Maybe chat for a bit and that.'

Kirsten gave a wry smile. A large part of her did. She wanted to get out and spend the evening in the company of someone who would admire her. He would entertain her; he would make her feel good about herself again. But it wasn't going to happen.

'Sorry, Tom,' she said. 'You're probably about a year and a half too late, but for what it's worth, two years ago, I would probably have said yes. You have a good life.'

The lift stopped and the doors opened at her floor, and she gave the man a smile. Kirsten walked to her room and once inside, stripped off and stood underneath the shower. Every now and then she'd let the tears come. She was about to go to work. She needed her mind clear, clear from everything. Even clear from Craig.

Chapter 04

The next morning, Kirsten awoke with her hand reaching out beside her and finding an empty bed. She felt guilty at the thought that she wanted it to be occupied by someone and hadn't brought Craig specifically to mind. It was hard now to put him in that place, with the way he'd treated her, the way he'd spoken to her. She couldn't get away from the feeling that something inside him had died with his injuries. Something had fundamentally changed in him. Then again, not everything stayed the same in life. Her brother hadn't either, disappearing from her to a point where he didn't even recognise her. Some journeys were hard.

Kirsten rose and showered before taking her breakfast in the restaurant downstairs. The man from the previous night was there again, smiling at her. She didn't engage him, instead eating quickly, returning to her room, and leaving with her backpack. There was no luggage, just the backpack, small enough to be taken on a flight. Kirsten made her way through the Heathrow jungle until she departed on a large jumbo jet for Alaska.

She was located in Economy and decided to while away her time researching Kyler's Peak, looking to see what she could find on the internet about it. No doubt when she landed, it would take her a while to get through customs, and she wondered just how they would treat her. Would anyone step in to warn her off being on their soil? If she had still been in the service, she'd expect nothing. Maybe a watchful eye, but no indication they knew her, but now she was outside of it, they were more likely to make an approach.

The other thing she was going to do was check out the plane and the passengers on it. Having seen the man yesterday, both at the restaurant and when she boarded the plane in Inverness, looking at her in what she considered to be a very suspicious way, Kirsten wanted to make sure that there were no operatives here. Was she being tailed? She didn't see how or why. After all, it was an obscure call to Craig, but unsure of what she was getting herself into, Kirsten decided to operate by the book and check out her fellow travellers.

It was about two hours into the flight when she took her first stroll. Wandering around Economy, looking but finding no one of particular interest, she then slipped up into business, telling the stewardess that she was there to say hello to a friend before coming back down. As Kirsten walked through, she glanced around and then nipped into first class, where she had to explain that she was lost when challenged by a steward. When she walked back down the other side of the aircraft through business, Kirsten saw him, the man from Inverness Airport, the man whose face was outside the restaurant. He turned away when she looked at him and as she walked past, she looked down to see what baggage he had with him. There was very little, and he was drinking.

Kirsten returned to her seat in Economy and sat down to watch a film, but her eyes were peeled on the doors ahead

25

of her, waiting to see if the man would come through. Sure enough, he appeared briefly, and for the next four hours, at half hour intervals, he would watch to see what she was doing. The flight to Anchorage was going to be a good nine and a half hours in total. Now, three-quarters away through the flight, Kirsten was still musing on the man's purpose.

Was he simply a tail? If so, why bother to come and see if she was still in economy? She couldn't get off the plane; after all, there were no parachutes. You couldn't kick the door open and just pop out. All he'd have to do was call up and make sure someone was in Anchorage when she arrived. Ted Stevens airport was an international airport with decent security. It wouldn't be that easy for her to slip away, not until she got clear of airside. If she vanished before passing out into the hall, they would realise that the passenger was missing airside. All hell would break loose.

Maybe he was here to warn her off. Maybe he was here to dispatch her. To simply watch her seemed wrong. Kirsten waited until there was an hour left in the flight and the next occasion she saw him look through from Business, she stood up and made her way to the rear of the plane to the toilets. One was available, but she waited, allowing the man to get closer. As she saw him walk into the rear section of the plane, she opened a vacant toilet door and stepped inside. There was no one else at the rear of the plane and as she anticipated, he caught the toilet door from being closed and stepped into the cubicle behind her.

She heard the door snip locked, but she drove an elbow straight into his gut, then turned, grabbing him by the throat. She spun round and planting him onto the toilet seat before hitting him hard several times in the face, but at the side so as

26

not to bloody his nose. She tapped him with a muscle relaxant stored inside a ring finger and watched as he flopped. It was good for keeping him quiet but making him talk would be awkward.

'What's your name?' she said quietly to him, standing astride him as he lay back on the toilet seat. 'I said what's your name?' She drove her finger in hard, touching a nerve that caused him to spasm even though he was flopped out. 'I can keep doing that,' she said.

'Suburba,' said the man. One of the problems with getting a dose of relaxant is you were never sure just quite how badly the person would react to it. It was there to incapacitate someone rather than prepare them for an information-gathering session. She would rather have injected him with other drugs that would affect the mind but she couldn't have restrained him without the relaxant where he was, certainly not easily.

For several minutes, Kirsten asked him questions, poking him to cause a reaction, to cause pain, but the man couldn't speak properly. She opened his jacket, and pulled out a passport that said Wayne Jenkins. She looked at the man's features. If anything, he looked South Mediterranean. There was a tan to him and almost a Roman nose. Other papers inside showed receipts, mainly food. There was no gun on him, no knives but then again, getting onto a plane with those would not be easy.

Kirsten looked at the man's ticket, but it gave no onward destination. He was flying into Anchorage and that was it. There was no indication also when it would have been booked. Just simply his business class seat. Economy was almost full, so maybe he hadn't been able to get into Economy. Maybe he didn't know where she was going and therefore, he'd just taken the middle end of the plane. It was a reasonable thought.

She now had a man totally relaxed, who had come to either extract information from her or possibly to kill her. She didn't want to break cover, but she couldn't haul him up to the authorities. She checked her watch. It was less than an hour's flight time. Maybe she could cause a diversion. Maybe she could cause him to need treatment. Make him the issue. She reached into the man's pockets again and found some paracetamol tablets.

She grabbed his head, moving it over and putting it underneath the tap of the small sink. The water from it could just about reach inside his mouth. She took out the paracetamol tablets, tossing the packet onto the floor before pouring them down into his mouth and making sure he swallowed every single one. If they came in and found him in this state, then they'd think he'd had an overdose. There were less than twenty tablets down him. It shouldn't kill him. By the time they'd realise what was going on, the muscle relaxant would've worked off. It was her best bet. They'd get him to the hospital; she'd get off the plane and disappear. If needs be, she could always leave the country by a different means.

Kirsten looked at her watch and it was half an hour until touching-down time. She listened carefully at the door. There was a usual commotion of people racing to the toilet before they landed, but in a quiet moment, she stepped out, closing the door behind her. Quickly, she made her way back to her seat, a roundabout route, taking the wrong aisle back to it, popping in across the top of Business and back down.

It was five minutes later when she heard the commotion at the back of the plane. She turned to see a stewardess rushing to grab a colleague. They made their way to the rear of the plane. A few moments later, there was a request on the cabin Tannoy for a doctor. Kirsten sat back in her seat as if she didn't care but occasionally looking over along with the rest of the passengers, ogling what was going on.

Kirsten reached out at one point as a stewardess rushed past. 'What's happening?' she said. 'Is everything all right?'

'We've just had someone collapse,' said the stewardess. 'It's okay. He's going to be all right, but we'll be getting him off as soon as we land. We need to get the cabin ready because we'll be touching down soon. We're getting a straight-in approach. There's nothing to worry about. The doctor thinks he'll be fine.'

Kirsten almost asked for more detail, but that would be unusual. She thanked the stewardess and sat back.

She scanned the rest of the economy class passengers as they came in, but no one seemed to be taking undue interest in her or more than passing interest in what was happening at the rear of the aircraft. All passengers were asked to remain seated after the aircraft had landed and taxied to stand. A team of paramedics raced on board, taking the poor man out from the toilets where he'd apparently collapsed and off to a waiting ambulance.

Shortly after, Kirsten and the rest of the passengers were allowed to disembark. As they exited, she stood in a queue for what seemed like over two hours to get through customs. Maybe someone was looking at her, she didn't know, but the queue moved slowly. When she arrived, she was asked why she was there.

'Holiday,' she said. 'Getting away for a couple of weeks.' Where would she go? Kirsten replied she was going to hire a car and head north up into the snowy wilderness for a while.

29

She was asked if she had enough money and she pulled up some bank account details showing she could look after herself and advised that she'd be back out of the country in about two weeks.

The man questioning her seemed satisfied, handed her back her passport, and Kirsten left the terminal building. She found a hire car company, spent fifteen minutes filling in paperwork before being shown to the car and driving out of the airport. *Cars here are bigger*, she thought. *They don't have wee cars like we do. Everything's bigger.*

She left Anchorage after buying a warm coat, the city behind her, and struck out on the long road up to Kyler's Peak. Her eyes checked the road behind, but she couldn't see anyone following her.

Two hours later, she stopped at a small café situated beside the road, ordered eggs over toast, and sat quietly eating. She looked around her, but there was no one interested in her. Well, except for a couple of young lads that cast a glance towards her, but that didn't bother her. What did bother her was she was happy. She'd been on the plane taking care of business with someone who'd been nosy, and now was on the open road about to investigate a problem. Yes, she was happy. As much as she cried for Craig, as much as she cried for the life she had back home when she'd held onto Macleod, a day and a bit later, she was happy. She didn't find the will in her heart to chastise herself for that.

Chapter 05

Kirsten continued north through Alaska until she was a good five hours clear of Anchorage out into the wilds of the country, although she hadn't strayed far from the main route. Now, she would turn off only slightly to the town of Kyler's Peak. She was tired. After all, their day was somewhat behind hers, so everything felt at the moment like it was late evening, very late evening, even though it was barely into the afternoon.

The town seemed somewhat elongated, spread out for the reported fifteen thousand people who lived in it. There wasn't anything high rise, all buildings only two or three stories high at the most, and yet some of the buildings were old. There was a history to the place, and she could see the historical museum with banners of people mining on display. There were certainly plenty of mountains around, including Kyler's Peak from which the town took its name which, according to the map, was a good half mile outside the town. A local attraction, albeit one with a rather bleak past.

Kyler had been a prospector, one who when all the money had run out, had taken a leap from the peak. That was colourful local history, but it wasn't important, and Kirsten's eyes were firmly fixed as she drove through town to where the local police station was. She was well out of her comfort zone. Back home, the police could always be influenced, well, at least when she was working for the service. They worked hand in hand, and while you didn't give them good reason to get involved, if they did, you could always clean things up. Here she was on foreign soil just like when she was back in Zante. The difference was here she wasn't the victim but rather merely someone investigating without a license.

The hotel she checked into was positioned beside a picturesque river, and in the current snow that surrounded the entire town, Kirsten found it breath-taking as the river wandered along, cutting under, here and there, the ice that occasionally formed across it in the calmer parts of its flow. Standing outside the car, which she had parked in a compact space despite the fact that she thought that it was quite large, she breathed in deep lungfuls of cold air.

It was very different weather to Scotland, although the temperature was low and yes, it was cold, it did feel like a different kind of cold. It didn't have that driving wet rain with the wind that numbed you to the core. That being said, she was sure it would be inadvisable to stay out here too long or to get lost out there in the wild. This cold could kill, as sure as staying out through the night soaked on a highland mountain.

The one thing that had struck Kirsten, and which was playing on her mind as she signed into the hotel, was that the town seemed to have so many lorries passing through it. It was positioned just off the main road and back home there would've been a bypass, so as not to heavily influence the town. Instead, she noticed that most of the semis, as they called them, passed through, stopping in various parts of the town.

The man behind the desk took her passport, examined her signature, and smiled, and asked her what she was doing so far north.

'I'm just exploring,' said Kirsten. The man looked at her hand baggage, the ruck slung over her shoulder.

'Don't have much with you,' he said.

'No,' said Kirsten. 'Travelling light as it's easier to see my way around.'

'How long are you going to be here?' asked the man.

'Oh, you booked up?'

'No,' he said. 'We'd just like to know. We can accommodate you quite easily and I was wondering how far in advance you'd like to pay.'

'You'd better book me in for three or four days,' said Kirsten. 'I thought I might take a walk up to Kyler's Peak someday. The internet had quite a story on it.'

The man smiled. 'It is quite the sight, but I'd be careful up there at this time of year. Be careful anywhere outside of the town with the snows if you're not used to them. You English people are often exploring; that's the way you are.'

'It's all right,' said Kirsten. 'I'm Scottish.'

She hadn't meant to say it with so much pride and in truth, she didn't have anything against the English, but it always riled her being called one. Dom was English, her partner in the service, and both he and Carrie-Anne were more than professional to work with. *Decent people too*, she thought as they had come to help her when she was out on her own.

'Oh, by the way,' she said to the hotel owner, 'can you tell me where the local paper is?'

'Local paper? You mean the *Kyler's Times*?' he asked. 'What do you want with them?'

'Local stories,' said Kirsten. 'Newspapers and that, they always have a scoop behind the tall tales, don't they? I thought they might have some of the old papers so I can get a little bit more history.'

'The museum's good for that,' said the man. 'Most people seem to manage in there.'

'Yes,' said Kirsten, 'but I thought I might even write a book about my travels, so I need to look for something a bit beyond just what the museum has. You need to be different, don't you? Try and stand out.'

'I suppose you do,' said the man. 'Breakfast is served from six to ten in the morning. I hope you have a pleasant stay with us. Have a good rest of your day.'

'You, too,' said Kirsten, and strode off to her room.

Once inside, she lay down on the bed only briefly, taking a moment to soak in what she would need to do. The room was very simple: a double bed, a bath, and shower room off to one side. There was a TV and a coffee maker. She looked at the free packets of coffee that came with it and wondered what Macleod would think of them. He'd probably chuck them in the bin and bring some of his own.

Coffee here was different as well. She thought the ones she'd drunk on the drive up, Java, was more bitter than what she was used to. It packed a bit of a kick. That was America though, wasn't it? She didn't dislike them, but they packed a bit more of a kick than other people. Not as smooth, more in your face. That had its benefits and its drawbacks, she thought. Kirsten didn't unpack anything but left her bag behind as she walked out to the car and then drove for the *Kyler's Times*, which was situated on the main street.

The hour was fast approaching five o'clock and she wondered if anyone would still be there. On arrival, she realised that the paper was not a big affair. It seemed to only have a single room facing the street. Maybe there was more in the back and upstairs although she wasn't hopeful. A single man sat peering over his glasses at a screen in front of him.

Kirsten knocked the door and saw him glance up before waving her in. The inside of the *Kyler's Times* was a mass of papers with three computers, each sitting on a different desk. The walls had plenty of pictures and copies of the paper, the occasional one being framed as if it was more splendid than the rest.

'Can I help you?' queried the man, peering over his black-rimmed glasses.

'I'm sure you can. My name's Kirsty. Kirsty Jameson.' It was the name on her false ID. It wasn't the name on the passport she'd used to enter the country. She'd only be there a few weeks. Kirsten thought if anybody was following her or just checking through later where she had been, she'd be out of the country by the time they were able to realise. She wasn't looking for trouble, but a girl was missing.

'Well, pleased to meet you,' said the man. 'How can I help you, Kirsty?'

'I'm actually here to talk to you about Melissa. I believe one of my colleagues has spoken to you previously.'

'It's a shame,' said Martin. 'She was a good girl, Melissa. We're not quite sure what's happened to her. Probably run off.'

'What happened exactly?'

'It's like I told your friend for the family. She just didn't come in one day,' said Martin. 'Just gone.'

'Is that her desk over there?' Kirsten pointed to one beyond Martin.

'Yes, that's where she sat, but she was always out and about.'

Kirsten drifted over towards the wall. She saw articles on it written with Melissa M. Carson as the legend at the bottom. There seemed to be a rather large number of them.

'Did she put these up or did you?'

'Oh, I did. She sure could write.'

'She was clearly busy, but I note that your desk is a lot busier looking than hers.'

'That's one of the things,' said Martin. 'She took a load of her notes with her. I wonder, was she off trying to sell a story elsewhere?' The man didn't look convinced of this.

'What do you think happened to her?' asked Kirsten.

'Well, I don't know, Kirsty, but I'll tell you something. I wouldn't go looking too deeply.'

'How do you mean?'

'Well, it's rattled the place a bit. Sheriff is interested. You learn over the years as a newspaperman when to get your nose back out.'

Kirsten sat on the edge of the man's desk leaning over, close to him. She often found with men that getting closer sometimes made them talk more. Whether it was because they were trying to impress you, or they just liked the soothing voice of a woman, she didn't know. In the service you learned to use whatever was at your disposal. If that happened to be your sexuality, then so be it.

'I wouldn't want to see someone like you get hurt,' said Martin quickly.

'Why would I get hurt? What was she into? What was she looking into at the time?'

'Just local stories. There wasn't much to it. She certainly didn't have anything here in the office that would indicate that she would do a runner. Maybe she stored some of it out at her own house.'

'You've been out there?' asked Kirsten.

'No,' said Martin. 'Sheriff has locked it off. Didn't want anybody into it. You don't rub the sheriff up of the place where you live. It's not a good idea, especially when you want to live here for a lot longer. He's quite a firm sort of man, likes his own way. Likes to be on top of things.'

'Have they got anywhere?'

'Not that they've told me, and they haven't told her family, I guess. They won't have got far. I wouldn't rub that in, either.'

'Maybe I'll take a spin out, Martin,' said Kirsten. She turned to walk to the door and then stopped. 'What is it with all these lorries?' she said to him.

'Lorries?' asked Martin. 'What do you mean, lorries?'

'Semis. Articulated lorries. Semis, that's what you'd call them, isn't it?'

'We're quite busy with that thing here.'

'Noticed a lot of them are refrigerated as well.'

'A lot of hog farms here. We're not just about mining. Cattle, hogs, got to make a living somehow. Not that most of the hogs will be out at this time of year. We bring them inside to the barns, but plenty of meat out here and about. Can't exactly grow lots of crops at the moment.'

Kirsten laughed. 'I guess you can't. Thanks for your time, Martin. You don't mind if I drop back in another time?'

'Did they send you to come and investigate?'

'Yes, Martin. They sent me to look at what was going on. Melissa's family are quite worried.'

'I told her when she started that she was working for a local paper and a local paper is here to support the community. You

37

don't have to get over-excited by what's going on. Just . . . ' Kirsten watched as the man's hands shook. 'You just keep your nose clean. It's a good life. Don't get a lot of hassle. Local people want to read about obituaries. They want to hear about the births in the town. They want to know when the next parade is. They're not interested in big dealings. *Kyler's Times* is a local paper.'

'She found something big, did she?'

'She didn't bring it all to me if she did. Maybe she thinks she has. Maybe she's trying to find another paper. I don't know what's going on with her. It's like I told the sheriff: one day she's here, the next she was gone.'

Kirsten watched the man closely, the little flicker in his face, the way his hands were slightly shaking. His foot, involuntary, moving back and forth underneath his chair. He was lying through his teeth, but she wasn't going to accuse him of it yet; she needed to know the lie of the ground. If Martin was afraid, the last thing she needed to do was scare him. His actions could lead to revealing who she really was, and right now, she didn't want to do that. It was one thing to pop along, to see what had happened to Melissa. It was quite something else to be an ex-agent, going to solve the matter.

Chapter 06

Kirsten stepped out of the newspaper offices and looked up and down the snowy street. It was becoming dark and snow was falling. She thought how at one time in her life, this could be the most picturesque thing going. Now, however, she was feeling cold and decided that she was probably hungry. Her system was knocked for six with the day being some six hours behind what she was used to. She could try and ring Craig, but in truth, she wasn't sure he wanted to hear from her. She wasn't sure if she wanted to bring that situation into her mind at present, not when she was so early to this serious situation and was still formulating about how to manage searching for Melissa.

First things first, she thought. *I need to get some food.* She walked through the town slowly until she saw a diner. Inside it looked over three-quarters full. Kirsten reckoned this was a good sign. There was a homeliness to it with wooden tables and chairs and an old neon sign flashing outside, saying 'Ma Gino's'. Despite the name, there was nothing Italian looking about it, and she saw the large American flag on the back wall and a number of combat-veteran photographs beside it.

That was another difference, she thought. *You wouldn't get that in the UK, not in a café or a restaurant.* Kirsten took her coat off and sitting down, noticed several people looking over at her. A couple of them gave appreciative nods towards her, and she wondered if these were the lonely middle-aged men of the town out eating on their own. She simply nodded back until she was interrupted by a young girl with an apron across her front.

'What can we do for you?' she asked. 'Are you ready to eat?'

The girl could only be sixteen, maybe eighteen, thought Kirsten, *and she's unbelievably cheery.*

'Something simple,' said Kirsten. 'I'm really hungry so a good plateful but something simple.'

'We can do pancakes; we can do eggs, a little bit of sausage with it.'

'Sounds good,' said Kirsten.

'You want syrup with that?'

Why not, she thought, *why not; when in Rome . . .*

The girl wrote down on her pad as Kirsten nodded. 'And what about a drink? Coffee? Some Joe?'

'What type of coffee is it?' asked Kirsten.

'What do you mean what type of coffee is it? It's black—you can put some milk in it if you want.'

'No, I meant where is it from?'

'It's from the delivery truck—brings us the coffee.'

'Just coffee then,' said Kirsten, feeling rather deflated. She sat in the chair looking casually around her until a large, older woman from behind the counter came along towards her and placed a knife and a fork down with a napkin. 'There you go, dearie. You from out of town?'

'Well, yes,' said Kirsten. 'My name's Kirsty Jameson. I'm over from Scotland. Just visiting, dropping by, and seeing your history and that. Just like to travel, you know?'

'Well, it's great to see you, Kirsty,' said the woman. 'Where are you staying with us?'

'A hotel down by the river.'

'All right. Alex looking after you down there?'

'Presume so. I didn't get his name.'

'Wife left him last year. You make sure you've got the only key to your room.' Kirsten looked up at the woman, slightly horrified, and then she waved her hand at her, 'I'm only messing with you. Alex is a good one, if a little bit lonely. See him in here a few nights a week. Don't get that good cooking like he used to. Boy comes for my cooking now.'

Kirsten watched as the woman put her hand on her hip, turned around, looking at some of the menfolk. She could see her give the odd wink at one or two of them. Kirsten tried to work out if this was who the woman was or whether she just put on an act when she served the customers.

'I'm Ma Gino; this is my place and you're most welcome, Kirsty. If we don't fill you up, you tell us, and we'll get you some more. I never see people go away from this establishment if they haven't been filled up. You'll probably not have a big appetite with how they eat in London.'

'I'm from Scotland,' said Kirsten. 'I think you'll find we have a decent appetite up there.'

'All right, you chasing ancestors then?'

'Something like that, popping in, seeing old friends along the way or at least daughters and sons of friends who were really friends with mum and dad.'

'That's good. Ah, here's your coffee. Annie's a good girl. You put that coffee down for Kirsty here. A decent mug for you too.'

41

It was a large mug and she sipped the coffee but almost spat it out when she tasted how bitter it was. It wasn't the best she'd had by a long stretch. She thought about talking about Melissa the moment she came in, about whether she could find her, but she wasn't convinced with Ma Gino. The woman was over the top, too over the top. It was a very public place to talk about things.

Ma Gino sat down and continued to bombard Kirsten with all sorts of details about the town. Most of them were fairly random, talking about good stores to go to, and where she could see some nightlife.

'Girl like you, are you clean living? You don't look it if you don't mind me saying. You certainly can turn a head in that outfit, but I bet you've got better outfits than that. Just watch the bars you go into, okay? Some of the guys up here, they're truckers and a bit rough. They're decent people but don't lead them on.'

Kirsten was quite taken aback by the forwardness of the woman, but she simply nodded and thanked her. A large plate of pancakes, fried eggs, and flat sausage arrived. Kirsten thought the sausage was more like a patty, not the square Lorne sausage she was used to at home, but she hungrily tore into it. Ma left her to return behind the counter.

As Kirsten ate, forcing the coffee down to wash the pancakes into her system, she noted Ma was on the phone. Through a couple of glances over at Ma, Kirsten could lipread the words 'woman', 'curvy' and 'unsure'. The rest of the time Ma turned, making it difficult to even guess at what she was saying.

Five minutes later, Kirsten had finished her plate and when Annie took it away, she went to down the rest of her coffee but found a chair at her own table being pulled out and a man in a sheriff's outfit sitting down.

'You don't mind me sitting down and welcoming you to Kyler's Peak?'

'I don't,' said Kirsten, rather taken aback.

'Annie,' the man shouted over. 'Come and fill up this coffee cup. It's on me.'

'Thanks,' said Kirsten, 'you don't need to do that.'

'Got to show a bit of hospitality to those from abroad. Where are you from? Scotland?'

It dawned with Kirsten that Ma Gino had spoken to the sheriff.

'Funnily enough.'

'Which part of Scotland?'

'The north, Inverness. Do you know it?'

'I'm not sure I do. What's your name there?'

'Kirsty. Kirsty Jameson.' Kirsten held out her hand and let the man shake it.

'Well, I thought I should come and say hello to you but give you a bit of a warning about the town. There's plenty of pleasant places like this, Ma Ginos, during the day, the shops and that, but our bars might not be like your bars. You look like a decent woman. There's a couple of them are a bit rough.'

'Ma was telling me,' said Kirsten.

'And you, well, don't take this the wrong way, but you'll turn a few heads. It's okay if you can turn a few heads and look after yourself, but some of these guys don't take no for an answer. It's not right. Well, we have words when it happens, but I wouldn't want you getting into that situation.'

'Well, that's very decent of you,' said Kirsten, 'but I can handle myself. Been on my own for a while.'

'I'm sure you can. It's just a friendly bit of advice. What are you doing here anyway, Kirsty?'

'Checking up on a friend's relative, passing through and travelling a bit too.'

'What friend's relative would this be?'

'Melissa. Melissa Carson. I got a work address, but I didn't get where she lived.'

The sheriff put his arms down on the table and took his hat off.

'Sorry to say Melissa's missing,' he said. 'Quite a serious case because we haven't seen her for a while. Personally, I think she's run off. Bit of trouble at the paper and that, but until we find out the truth of it . . .'

'What is the truth of it?' asked Kirsten.

'We don't know yet. We're still looking and wondering, but you need to be aware that it's not a great situation. People gone for this long, hopefully, they've done a runner. Hopefully, they're just getting out. I think there was a bit of friction at the paper. Closed off her house though. It's a crime scene.'

'Did something happen there?' asked Kirsten.

'No, but it's evidence. Plan to go through all her stuff.'

'Okay. Can I help at all? I didn't know her very well, but I just thought I could help if you need me to.'

'It's okay. Let the professionals take care of this.'

A cup of coffee arrived at the table from Annie, one in each hand, and she placed one before the sheriff and one before Kirsten.

'Don't think me rude,' said Kirsten, 'but what are you doing, exactly, to find Melissa?'

'Well, all we can; we're putting everything into it. Don't worry about that. I'm more worried about you out here on your own. It's like every town. We have darker places here.

You need to be very careful.'

'So you've said.'

'Being a friend of Melissa's, well, if she hasn't run off and it's something else, you know what these weirdos are like, end up going for a friend of the woman they've already, well, let's not go there. That's a bit of a dark thought, but you need to be careful.'

'I can handle myself.'

'Really? Have you got a weapon?' asked the sheriff.

'No. Do I need a weapon? We don't normally carry weapons where I come from. Besides, weapons are only good enough if the brain behind them is up to the task. Last thing I need to do is pull a trigger over here and have you all over me. If you don't know firearms, best not to touch them.'

'That sure is true,' said the sheriff. 'Look, no disrespect to you, Miss Jameson, but don't get involved. We're doing what we can. We'll tell her family what we know when we get there. If somebody's done wrong to her, we'll lock him up. If she's done a runner, she'll turn up. Don't get in the way and get yourself into a mess. Seen it too often. We know what we're about and I wouldn't want to see you get harmed.' His hand reached forward and touch Kirsten's. 'You sure are a pretty wee thing, aren't you?'

Kirsten watched as he studied her and then withdrew her hand quickly. 'But trust me, I can look after myself, pretty or not,' said Kirsten. 'Thank you for the advice. If I need you, I know where to call.'

'Don't be afraid to, and of course if you come across anything about Melissa you think is relevant to the case, please pop in and see me. Be an absolute pleasure to have you in the office. Time don't wait for me though. Got to get back to the job. It has been a delight meeting you though.'

'Thank you for your hospitality,' said Kirsten, although she gave the statement a cold feel. The sheriff doffed his hat and then exited the café. Kirsten noticed that his coffee was only half drunk and she hadn't touched her own second cup. She took out some cash, left it on the table, and exited out into the cold air.

Night had truly fallen, but the street lamps made sure that everything could be seen. She watched the townsfolk traipse here and there, but over the road she saw the sheriff in his car looking through the window. It was clear he was watching her. Some people might have thought he simply liked staring at a good-looking woman, but Kirsten saw the stare. It was much more than that. He knew more than what he was saying, and not just about Melissa, but about her too.

Chapter 07

The walk back from the diner to her car was conducted on snowy sidewalks and across wide roads. A few times Kirsten felt her footing was unsure, but she used the opportunity to look around her, as if she was stumbling or slipping. As soon as she'd left the cafe, a young man had been on her tail. He was maybe in his early twenties and he clearly hadn't done this sort of work before, for he was easily spotted. She walked here and there around streets she barely knew and found it quite easy to lose him amongst the evening folk returning home from work. By the time she got into her hire car, he was nowhere in sight.

The police sheriff had said that the house was out of bounds. Kirsten wasn't too sure where it was. The edge of town had been described. Kirsten pulled into a gas station and asked the young teller where the missing girl had lived. The story about her was a bigger one than Kirsten had expected but then again, the town was much smaller than she had first thought. Someone disappearing amongst ten to fifteen thousand people would be a big deal, especially when they worked for the local press.

The attendant at the gas station told her that the house was out on the edge of town, quite separate from many others. Kirsten followed the roads out and drove past the house when she saw a police car sitting outside. Having lost her, they must have reckoned on where she would end up, but even in the dark, Kirsten thought she could get past their watchful eyes.

She parked the car over a mile away, off road and under some trees. When she got out with her coat and gloves on, she felt as if she should have another three or four layers on top of them to keep herself warm. She walked quickly, generating enough heat underneath the thermal coat she had bought at the airport. The property was close to a small, wooded area and there was only a fifty-yard run to the back door from the trees that Kirsten spied the house from. The police car was still at the front. She almost laughed when she saw the young deputy in the front seat consuming doughnuts.

She was also sensible enough to scout the area to see if anyone else was watching. There was no one and so she made a beeline for the rear door of the property out of sight of the police car parked at the front. They surely didn't know who she was then, for if they had known she was a former British secret agent, they wouldn't have put a young deputy out front to spy.

There was tape across the back door and Kirsten peeled it and then used her lock picks to open the rear door. She had kept them after leaving the service. They could be discreetly hidden in hand luggage, hard to detect, and were most useful. The house was dark inside but there were windows to the front, and she made sure to stay in the shadows. The house was smart, with a modern kitchen that was clean. However, there were several dishes sitting on one side. *Not something you do if you plan to go away. Maybe she'd run. Maybe there wasn't time or maybe she'd been taken.*

Kirsten checked the fridge and saw foods going out of date. Beside the kitchen was a small office. She looked through the papers there but Kirsten saw very little evidence of Melissa's work. There were bills from the electric company, the gas company too, but nothing from the paper.

The computer in front of her was obviously a well-used one for there were pads and pens around it but none of them were written on. She thought about firing the computer up but the light from the screen would show through the windows at the front of the house and she couldn't very well close the curtains. That would be a dead giveaway to what she was doing. As it was, she shone a small pen torch around.

She saw some photographs and then one caught her. One of Craig. He was a bit younger than he was now and he was holding a baby with two besotted parents at the side of him. Kirsten held the photograph for a moment and felt a tear coming to her eyes. She wanted to ring him. She wanted to tell him how she felt but she remembered the anger he had towards her. 'Space,' he'd said. He needed space. Maybe he did.

She suddenly jumped when she heard a sound. Carefully, she crossed the room and looked at the rear garden and saw a moose which had kicked over a bin at the rear. Kirsten remained in the shadows then made her way into the front living room looking at the young constable beyond. He was oblivious, deep in heavenly flavour with his doughnuts and possibly reading a book.

When she went upstairs, she found many clothes left behind, and a bed that was unkempt but not slept in. *She hadn't tidied up before she left. Had she been intending to come back? There*

49

was no evidence of work. If something had been on her mind if she had been investigating something, would she have left it around the house? If she knew they were coming for her, what would she do?

It was pure speculation but if it had been Kirsten, she'd have found somewhere to put it. Somewhere out of the way. That was part of a journalist's work, wasn't it? Keep your source material separate. She'd been brought up with that surely. She wouldn't have it all at the paper. If she was such a threat, she might be a brighter girl too.

Kirsten checked the house for the tell-tale signs of a secret hiding hole. She pushed walls and she lifted the carpet, scanning the floorboards, but nothing came to sight. Carefully she went through every room checking fixtures until she saw it. The computer was plugged into a socket with an old three-style pin American socket. That didn't look unusual except this was a reasonably new build and the plug socket was off kilter. She could see where the wall had been painted originally and the plug socket had been moved at an angle so that there was a slight run of bare wall where paint hadn't been applied.

Kirsten took out a penknife and unscrewed the fixture, pulling it back from the wall. As she did so, a small key fell onto the floor. Kirsten replaced the fixture before picking the key up, hunkering down in the kitchen, and shining a light on it. It looked like a locker key, some bus station key, for there was a logo and no words, but simply a bus drawing on it. The number 132 was on the side of it.

Kirsten pocketed the key deciding she'd done about as much as she could and left via the back door. As she crept back into the forest, she saw the snow continuing to fall, thankful that her tracks would very shortly be covered. Once back in her car, she turned the heating up full, suffering from the chill. She wondered what she should do next.

As she'd lost her tail, the police sheriff would be wondering what her movements would be. Maybe he'd be back at the hotel waiting for her to come in. Maybe he'd be checking bars. The she got the idea of a simple cover.

It was fast approaching midnight. Kirsten drove into town, parking her car up before entering what looked like the roughest bar she could find. She had left her coat in the car, and marched into the bar in a black T-shirt, dark jeans, boots, and ordered a shot of whiskey. As she stood there, a man came up beside her, putting his hand on her hip.

'Let me get that for you, darling.'

'Why not?' said Kirsten.

For the next two hours, she sat with the man, letting his hands roam around her back down towards her bottom. She even kissed him a few times. When she went to leave at two o'clock, he followed her outside but when she went to grab her coat from the car, he grabbed her arm pulling her to one side. She let herself be dragged down into an alleyway, where the man clearly wanted to receive something for the drinks he had paid for. It took a moment for Kirsten to drill a knee up into his stomach and let him fall to the ground. He was so drunk that he'd probably barely remember the evening, and he certainly wouldn't tell everyone a woman he'd picked up had simply dropped him in an instant.

Kirsten walked back to the car, took out her coat, made sure the car was locked, and headed for the nearest taxi. It was a bit of a walk because at two in the morning, and in a town this size, there weren't many about, but she dropped into one of the bars, and they soon sorted one for her. Just after three in the morning, she stepped out of the taxi at the front of the hotel. As she went to enter, she saw the sheriff coming out from inside.

'I thought I told you to take care of yourself. I told you this town wasn't like where you come from.'

'You're right. You can't hail a taxi here, and your whiskey's different. It's not the same at all.'

'Kirsten, don't mess me about. I'm concerned for your safety.'
Concerned you couldn't tail me, more like, thought Kirsten.

'I told you I'm fine,' said Kirsten, faking a slur in her voice. 'I just need to go to bed. I had one of the guys get a little bit excitable, but I saw him off. It's not a problem.'

'Let me escort you into your room,' said the sheriff.

'There's no need for that. No need at all. You shouldn't have come out here so late, waiting, and looking for me. Did you think I was missing?'

Kirsten looked into the man's eyes. They almost seemed to be in a rage. He got the taunt.

'You left your car in town then. Maybe I could go and bring it back for you?'

'I'll get it tomorrow. Don't worry, I don't drink and drive, very big on that back home. Taxis are the way to go. If you don't mind, I'd like to get to bed.'

'Where exactly were you?'

'The bar.'

'We didn't see you in the bar all evening.'

'Which bar did you go to then?' asked Kirsten. 'You really followed me around?'

'We're just concerned about your safety, but we didn't see you in any of the bars.'

Kirsten made a stumble towards him, put a finger up to her lips. 'Got a bit of action, Sheriff. Don't tell anyone. Don't want to give the impression I'm that kind of woman.'

She watched as he grunted and strode past her to the police car that was sat outside the hotel. Kirsten continued the image of a drunk woman until she got inside her room. Once there, she made for the shower to wash off what she'd had to do that evening; several hours of being talked at and having your back, hips, and bottom fondled, but it had been worth it. Worth it for the key she'd found.

Now, in the morning she'd go to the bus station. She'd have to be clever about how she did it. They knew she wasn't who she said she was, but they couldn't prove it for now. If she gave them more and more of a run-around, maybe they would come after her. Maybe. Anyway, she was in the clear for the rest of the morning.

At four o'clock, she crawled in under her bed covers, and she thought about reaching for the phone. Could she even do that though? Maybe they had tapped her hotel phone. After all, the sheriff had put someone on her, someone to trail her. He knew she was somebody. Maybe he didn't know who she was, for his intelligence was poor. One thing she did know; Melissa was onto something, and she knew it. The key might show what it was she was onto. The sheriff also knew something else, and Kirsten would have to find out just exactly what his involvement with Melissa was.

Chapter 08

The following morning, Kirsten rose and just about made breakfast before the ten o'clock deadline at the hotel. She threw some bagels, scrambled eggs and bacon in her before returning to her room and showering again. Even seeing the snow outside made her cold, but she found herself warming up in her room by doing some quick high knees, squat thrusts, and other exercises. Ready to face the day, she put her coat on, the bus station key in her shoe and walked to the front of the hotel where she watched for anyone leaving.

A woman was making her way towards her car, and Kirsten stopped her, asking where she was going. She explained that she had left her own car in town last night, because she'd had a drink and wondered if the woman could drop her there. Despite looking a little put out, the woman agreed, and Kirsten was soon in the middle of town without having to call for a taxi or give away her movements.

The bus station was in the middle of town and Kirsten walked round it several times trying to spot anyone watching her. There was no one there. After waiting for an hour to guarantee that no one was in attendance, she walked to where the lockers were in the main foyer of the station. She looked along, saw what looked like a beaten-up row with several lockers left lying open, but towards the end, locker 132 was intact. Kirsten went to the toilet, at the far end of the station and inside the cubicle, took out the key from her shoe.

Returning to the locker, she tried the key, found the locker opened and pulled the door back slightly ajar. Inside was a rucksack. Kirsten glimpsed around again, wondering how she would get it out if someone was watching her, but knew that now she'd opened the door, she needed to move quickly. Before she moved however, she unzipped the rucksack and looked inside. There were papers, nothing but sheets of paper. She estimated maybe thirty to thirty-five. Kirsten zipped the bag back up, pulled it from the locker and slung it over her shoulder, closing the locker door behind her and locking it again.

As she turned away from the locker, her eye caught a figure on the far side of the bus station. She had seen the same figure last night, eating donuts while sitting outside Melissa's house. How had he known she was here? Did they have people on the lookout or people phoning in to the station from the townsfolk? She hadn't been followed down, and although she hadn't been overly discreet, yet hiding her approach to the bus station, she didn't think she'd given herself away in any particularly overt fashion. There must be people calling into the sheriff's office. Did he have people at the bus station? Was it the hotel manager?

Kirsten couldn't worry about that. She had what she needed. Now she needed to get out and get somewhere safe to read the documents that were inside the bag over her shoulder. As she strode across the bus station, she watched the younger man follow her. Again, he was poor at it, for it was so obvious what he was doing, but she now had evidence of some sort which may explain what Melissa was doing.

It was clear that the sheriff had something to protect in the investigation and Kirsten would need to know what that was. The sheriff, however, had shown himself to be quite a forward man, and she wasn't sure that if he was threatened that he would talk easily. Instead, she wondered if she caught this man who was tailing her in such a bad fashion, maybe he would blurt out what was going on. He didn't look to be someone worth their salt for the job he was doing.

Kirsten exited the bus station, milling in the crowd and almost lost the young man. She was able to watch him from around the corner as he desperately looked for where she was. She walked back out and let him follow her.

She thought it best if she let him tail her away from where he'd originally picked her up, just in case he had called for any assistance. As she walked on, she began to spy the best place to have a conversation with him and realised that one of the back alleys behind the main shopping area was particularly dark and looped away so it couldn't be seen from the main street. Kirsten did a circular route and came back past the opening before heading down the alley. Once she made sure he was watching her at the entrance, she cut back into an alley that took away any view from the main street. It was about thirty seconds later, when he rounded the corner.

Kirsten grabbed his arm, drove it up behind his back and marched him to the end of the alley. He tried to struggle, but she was easily strong enough to hold him. Once at the end of the alley, she pushed him, so he bounced off the wall, and then she held him by the throat.

'Who are you? Talk,' she said.

'Don't, don't, I'm just . . . I'm just protecting you.'

'You're just protecting me? How in the world would you protect me?' asked Kirsten. 'You can't even tail me properly.'

'I'm just doing my job. I've been told. I'm a deputy. I'm the new deputy.'

'Who told you to tail me?'

'The sheriff. Sheriff told me that you had to be tailed. I was to watch out for you, said you were getting yourself into all sorts of trouble. He said last night that you would go to the house, the Carson house. I was to watch out for you there, but you weren't there.'

'No. I was out enjoying myself in the town. I met your sheriff when I came back at three in the morning. Why are you fellas watching me? Do you not get good-looking ladies in Kyler's Peak?'

The man's eyes swam. Kirsten could swear that there were tears coming to them. She wasn't holding his throat that tightly, but he certainly wouldn't be able to move away. She reached down, took a gun from inside his jacket, and threw it to the ground.

'I don't like weapons,' she said. 'Especially in the possession of someone that's gibbering the way you are. Who knows what you could do with one. Why is your sheriff so interested in me?'

'I'm telling you, he just told me where to go, to look after you. He said you'd be at the hotel this morning. When I got there this morning, you weren't there, or rather you hadn't got up. I was waiting but you came down here without me spotting you.'

Well, he obviously wasn't waiting in the car park all night, thought Kirsten. *That's something for him.*

'How did you trace me to here?' she asked.

'Because we have people who tell us. The hotel manager told me when you left. The bus station, Carly, at Information said you were here. That's when I came down. I was in town anyway. I'd known you'd come down. I wasn't far behind. Just watching out for you. Then you took that rucksack.'

'What about it?'

'Well, you got a rucksack. You haven't been here at the bus station. You opened the locker with a key. Did Melissa give you a key?'

'Why would you think Melissa would give me a key? I came here to find Melissa and she's not here.'

'No, she's not. She disappeared. It's worrying. She was . . .'

'She was what?'

'She was well-liked. She ran the paper. Well, I say ran. Martin runs it, but Martin's been doing papers for years and his stories are rubbish. She came and she wrote good stories and then she had a better story. That's what they say.'

'Who says?'

'People say. She must have had a better story, so she's legged it. She's gone, and maybe Martin didn't like that. That's the other thing.'

'What was the story about?' asked Kirsten.

'I don't know. I really don't know.'

Kirsten lifted the man up by the throat. 'You really don't know? Give me a guess.'

'There's talk of gold.'

'What talk of gold?'

'Gold mines but the mines are gone. The mines are no good anymore. That's what the place was raised on. That's why we are here but it was years ago, one hundred years ago, maybe one-fifty. Everybody always dreams around here that there's more gold, but there's not. That's why we farm now.'

'Has the sheriff got anybody else watching me?'

'No, we can't spare too many people. He said I should do it. I don't think he's that bothered. You said it. I'm not good at this. I'm just watching you. I'm not trying to be secretive about it. I'm trying to protect you.' Kirsten let the man's feet touch the ground.

'What are you going to do now? You going to call it into him and say, 'Oh look, she's onto me?''

'I have to tell him that. He'd want to know where you've been as well. They'll probably want to know what you've got with that backpack.'

'Maybe he will.'

'What is in it anyway?'

'You don't get to ask the questions yet. What's your name?'

'Greg. I'm Greg. Deputy Wiseman.'

'You better start living up to your name. I don't think your sheriff's going to be very happy and I've just pulled you in here. I did tell him I can look after myself. Anyway, Greg, I think the important thing here is that you get out of my hair.'

'I'm going to need to know what's in that bag.'

'No, you don't, Greg; understand that.' Kirsten reached down and picked up the gun and put it back into Greg's holster. 'You're a law officer and I'm not here to get into trouble with you, but you give me grief and I will stop you. You seem like a decent kid. You are still a kid, aren't you? You must only be about twenty-two.'

'I'm only three months in. You can't send me back like this. He'll be raging. He'll be absolutely . . .'

A shot rang out from the end of the alley. Kirsten watched Greg's head half explode and he toppled to the ground.

Kirsten wiped the human debris from her face and looked to the far end of the alley. There was a figure running. She reached down but Greg's eyes were cold. His body jittered, but there was no life to it for half the head was missing.

She spun around, looking at the alley. There was only one way out. *Should be about thirty seconds before people come running up*. The gunshot had reverberated around the alley and Kirsten looked for doors into the stores. She reached for his weapon, took out a handkerchief, and rubbed it down before dropping it in the alley. She then spotted a drainpipe, jumped onto it and began to climb up the outside of the building. She was able to swing across onto a fire escape, find a window, and force it open. By the time Kirsten was inside and had shut it, she saw figures arriving in the alley, staring down at the dead deputy. Greg Wiseman was no more.

Things had just escalated, but she didn't have time to think about that. Instead, she needed to get on the move. She looked around and realised that she was in a storeroom of some sort. Quickly she walked to the door, opened it, and saw a corridor outside. Someone was coming, so she shut the door quickly, heard them walk past, opened it again, and followed them down. At the end of the corridor, she saw a clothing rail with various smart cashier uniforms. She must have been in a department store and these were the outfits that many of them wore. She grabbed one, taking off her coat and putting the small jacket around her. Quickly she wiped her face down to remove any traces of the deceased Deputy Wiseman. Kirsten reversed her coat and then put it on a hanger and brought it with her like she was simply moving stock about.

She needed to get out into the shop quickly. Into the shop, and then back out onto the streets in a way. She could hear sirens wailing. The police would be all over the place soon.

Kirsten found stairs at the end of the corridor that seemed to lead down a couple of floors. The shop wasn't big, three floors at most. She soon reached the bottom and strode out onto the shop floor. She saw several of the staff and turned her back to them, walking out into the middle of the shop before crouching down behind a clothing unit. Once there, she stripped off the uniform, took her coat off the hangar, put it back on, stood up, and made straight for the doors.

As she did so, several policemen ran in and she quickly turned, pretending she was looking at some underwear in front of her. As soon as they'd run past to the rear of the shop, she turned, walked crisply but calmly out of the front door and back into the snowy street.

She walked across town away from the alley she'd been in, backpack still on making a circuitous route to see what the state of play was with the police. They seemed very tied up with what had gone on in the alley, so she made her way back to her own car. She threw the rucksack into the boot, jumped into the front, and drove out of town. Her heart was racing. Somebody had just shot a deputy. Somebody was serious about whatever she'd found. She needed to look inside that rucksack and find out what was going on.

Chapter 09

Kirsten was several miles out of town when she spotted a large barn. It was probably used for some sort of storage because it wasn't on any particular farm. Indeed, it seemed a distance from anywhere. Driving past, she pulled off the road into a large clump of trees obscuring the car from the view of any passing motorist. Satisfied her car was hidden, Kirsten walked through the wooded area in the deep snow and approached the barn from the rear. There was a small door secured with a lock which took her only thirty seconds to open. Once inside, she saw why the barn was deserted.

There were machines everywhere, wood choppers, grass cutters, and it took her a moment to count up the number of lawnmowers. *Was there a golf club near here?* she wondered. That must be what it was. You certainly couldn't play golf at the moment.

It had never occurred to her that there were parts of the world where golf was a seasonal thing. Back in the UK, it was played all year round, albeit probably better enjoyed in the summer months. What the barn gave her was comfort for surely nobody would be coming out here, not for a couple of months anyway. She would have time to stop, and she sat down in the corner pondering what to do.

She took off her coat and looked at it. She had reversed it, which was a great idea for escaping, but the blood that was on the inside of it needed washed. She was inside a facility for storing grass-cutting machines. There was hardly going to be a washing machine with a tumble dryer.

She looked down at the T-shirt she wore underneath. Thankfully it was black but it was also stained with blood, although she wasn't sure if that was from the coat having been reversed or if she had it open at the time?

Kirsten stripped the t-shirt off, checked her jeans, and noticed several splatters of blood on them too and quick quickly removed them also. She walked to the door of the barn, pushed it open, and shifted a large degree of snow from outside into the barn. After closing the door, she used the snow to rub down the t-shirt, the coat, and the jeans. It wasn't perfect, but it certainly diluted the stains. She would need to get them in the washer at some point or into a bath where the blood could soak out. The hotel would be perfect except there was another question ringing through her head.

Someone had shot the deputy. They were shooting from the far end of the alley. Who had the target been? Was it her or him, or was it a shot that was meant to scare and had gone badly wrong? There were too many questions. As she dressed back into her clothes, Kirsten stared at the rucksack that was at the centre of all this trouble.

The police would be a problem. After all, the deputy had been there to watch her and although she hadn't been seen with him except by the shooter, the fact that the man had reported he was following her would certainly cause problems. She

63

could expect to be hauled in. It looked like the hotel might be out of bounds for a while.

Kirsten switched on one of the interior lights of the barn and she tore open the rucksack. She felt chilled, especially after putting the wet clothes back on, but she didn't want to sit in her underwear in case she had to make a run for it if somebody came in.

Kirsten removed the papers from inside the rucksack and made a count of them. The total was thirty-two sheets, double-sided and she sat down to read them. In truth, the handwriting was a wild scribble as if the person was quickly wanting to catch every word that was being said. Kirsten could tell from the top of the paper, they had previously all been on a pad, then ripped off and she could see even the occasional page wasn't complete, a slight rip at the top. The other thing she noted about them was they were that lined paper, jotter paper, paper you would carry about with you if you'd been at college or work.

What was written on the paper was a conversation, one that went back and forth referring to a potential relook at an old mine. It didn't mention where it was, but the conversation flowed from one side explaining how the mine, although it had been surveyed and reported as being spent, was actually full of gold. The report of the mine state had been fabricated and the real one showed that rich deposits were there.

Kirsten scanned the document for a name but there was only one, Howlett's Mine, and it was ringed in pen. She took out her phone and searched up for a Howlett's Mine in the area. It indicated an area not far from Kyler's Peak. Kirsten continued her search to find out that Howlett's Mine had been listed amongst many others, years ago, back in the day when Kyler's Peak was first being established as a prospecting township. Much gold had been derived from it, until the mine was declared spent and the prospecting around it fell away.

There'd been some scuffle over land rights and the mine had lain dormant for a long time. Kirsten wasn't sure who had rights to it, or who was working it, for searches on the internet were not bringing up anything of detail.

She scanned back through the paper in front of her, seeing that Howlett's Mine was up for purchase. One party was indicating that it could be put to the market, and if so, the other party could purchase it. She read that the first party was not in a position to purchase it for they were there to see fair play done but that the other party would be able to, and there was a quid pro quo coming. The second party said they weren't interested in mining gold; said they didn't know how to do it and the first party told them that the business was on the turn. Soon, there wouldn't be much business around Kyler's Peak, but to revive the place, the gold would be useful, useful for more than just the money it would bring in. As the pair in the conversation got to discussing what this meant, the pages had run out.

Kirsten wondered if this was Melissa's writing, and she sent a message to her father asking him to send a sample to her through her email. As she sat in the cold pondering what the information in front of her meant, Kirsten wondered what her next move should be. She wanted to get back to the hotel. Was that wise?

She scanned through the news reports on her phone, which all reported the shooting of a deputy. There was no report of a woman with him, nor a report of her disappearing. Why should there be? Only the police knew she was being tracked.

Certainly, they couldn't be so stupid to think that she would take out someone of such prominence and with a gunshot so loud that would bring people running. What was the purpose of this killing?

Kirsten stood suddenly and began to pace. She needed to be on the move, or she needed to find some sort of heat within this lawnmower home. She walked around, stepping between multi-headed lawnmowers and larger machines, clearly there to cut down more substantial grass. She played out scenarios in her head.

Was somebody trying to frame her? If so, why? To get her out of Kyler's Peak? In that case, somebody else must have dealt with Melissa, or had they meant to shoot the deputy to keep the deputy off Kirsten's back? If that was the case, they were dumb. She was better than that, and they clearly didn't know who she was.

Who'd been the man watching her, the man she'd taken out on the plane? Somebody knew something about her. She needed to be careful with her next move though. If she went to the hotel and they simply arrested her, she could very easily be on a plane out of here or worse. They could try to stick a murder charge on her. She had no gun though, so it would be hard to trace a weapon to her. She cleaned the one that the policeman had on him.

Anyway, the bullet hadn't been fired from that weapon. It hadn't been shot at all. From that point of view, she was clear. *Clear* she thought, *I'm only clear if a hunt for the truth is what they're intending. Is the sheriff who he says he is.* She was abroad in an area she didn't know in a reconnaissance mission. It was quickly changing into something else.

Back with the service, it had been easy. If there was

66

somebody in the way of the mission you were doing, you took them out. The service didn't get overly upset as long as they weren't Joe Public, or any of the people you were investigating. They were just a casualty of the war. The service would cover it up. The service could have a word with the local police. The service could take over.

Not here. Here, she was in somebody else's territory. Here, she'd have to look after her own safety as well. Kirsten opened a small rear door and looked out. She could just about see the road from where she was, and as she watched closely, she saw lorry after lorry passing by. There seemed so many. All the time, trips back and forward.

Then again, that was Alaska, wasn't it? Somewhere like Anchorage at the centre and the rest of the country supplying, bringing in, exporting. There was a lot of movement of goods, so maybe it wasn't so ridiculous that this small town had so much activity around it. That was the thing, living in the UK, it was so compact by comparison; it truly was a different world.

Kirsten began to shiver. She turned and packed up the rucksack, with the pages inside, carefully locked up the lawnmower barn behind her, then walking through the snow. She got into the car, turned it on, and began to drive. She took a track that headed off the main road and drove round and round, letting the car engine turn over and the heater warm up the interior of the car.

It felt good, the hot air blasting through it, but she knew at some point she'd have to stop. She saw a sign for an old prospector's hut exhibition, but it was out of season. Regardless, she carried on down and found herself to be the only car in a heavily snowed car park.

She stopped the car, walked over to the exhibition, and found it to be locked. Touching the window, she understood there was heat inside. Kirsten looked around, found a rear door, and using her lock picks, broke in. Casually, she sat down and while it wasn't quite bliss, there was a level of warmth that the barn hadn't provided.

Once again, she took out the sheets of paper, laying them down in front of her, staring at them with the remainder of the day's light that was coming through the large window of the exhibition. As she read, she was two feet from a mannequin of an old prospector. His face showed a forced smile as gold was being found in front of him.

Gold would certainly be a motive for anybody. The idea that this mine had been misrepresented, if it went off to market, people would be paying no price at all. For what? More than that, maybe people wouldn't want it. You could acquire it without even having to bid against anyone. It would all be under the radar. Then what? Could you mine it and move it without people knowing or would it be okay to bring it back into the light?

Kirsten was aware that she did not understand quite what she was looking at, or just how much of a catch owning this mine would be. *How easy was it to cover up this report that misrepresented the mine? Who would be able to do it? Who would have to be in on it?*

She held the page in front of her with the name Howlett's Mine, ringed in pen. *Howlett's Mine,* she thought. It didn't even sound impressive. Maybe it was just the name of who had first found it, but for whatever reason, somebody had possibly killed a deputy over this. Melissa was missing. Had she run or was she simply a victim? And who was carrying out this potential fraud.

As dark fell around the exhibition, Kirsten thought about her next plan. Where should she go? Who should she talk to? Maybe she should return to the hotel. She was aware that the longer she stayed away, the longer she wasn't found, the less convincing her story that she hadn't been around the deputy would be. She could return to the hotel and face down the police. There was nothing on her. They weren't looking for her overtly. It was better that she knew if she had to run than playing this hanging-around game. It would be easier to investigate knowing that you could walk down the street, but she'd need to get into her room first or find somewhere else to clean off this blood, because at the moment, that was the only thing tying her to the death of the deputy.

Chapter 10

Rather than return direct to the hotel by the front door, Kirsten thought it better that she should check it out before announcing any arrival. She parked her car over a mile away and then walked through the snow, off the road, until she came to the edge of the hotel complex. It wasn't large, but from across the river, she was able to spot the police car sitting outside.

Clearly, they were waiting for her return, and she wondered if they'd already been inside checking through her belongings. They wouldn't find anything, as Kirsten wasn't dumb enough to leave anything in the room that could incriminate her and she had no weapons with her, trusting herself as the only weapon she would need. After all, she wasn't here to cause a stir, just to find out what was going on.

As she sat looking at the police car waiting for her, she pondered on her next move. If she went in now and they arrested her or took her in for questioning, she could be two or three days before she would see the outside of a cell. In her mind, it would seem totally unfair. If she gave a simple explanation, they would probably be obliged to release her, but this was Alaska, not Inverness.

What would happen if somebody from a service like she had been in, but from the Americans, took an interest? If her background was known, they could certainly keep her under wraps for a while. Her interest had been piqued by Howlett's Mine and she wanted to know more about it.

The paper's editor, Martin, had been brought up within Kyler's Peak, so he should know where all the details were kept about such things. He might even know about the mine itself. Kirsten realised she was in the dark not knowing if there was public knowledge about that particular mine or if it was more covert.

Taking a last glance at the river running along, she walked back in the dark to her car parked off road. She drove into town, leaving the vehicle in a car park and walked across town towards the offices of the paper. As she got closer, she saw a police car outside it as well. *Were they reading her mind?* Maybe they just knew where she'd been. After all, these were the people she'd talked to; the hotel she was staying in; Martin.

She glanced at her watch and realised that it was past six now. Maybe Martin would be making a move soon, although, with the deputy's murder, there would be plenty to put in this paper.

Kirsten found some cash and managed to obtain some hot takeaway food, walking around the town eating it, before coming back to the paper and waiting for Martin to leave. When he did so, she jumped onto the bus that he took and then watched as he got off amongst a small area of houses on the edge of town. She jumped off a stop later and strode back, hurrying so she could see him making his way along a small avenue.

At a house at the end, he opened the front door, switched

71

on the lights and entered. Kirsten could see no police car, but rather than go up to the front door in case the neighbours were watching, she scouted around through the wilds behind the houses and entered Martin's grounds by his rear garden. The snow was deep, her jeans were soaked, and she was cold, but at least she was unseen. Approaching his rear door, she saw that he was in the kitchen, but crept up, picked the lock on the back door, and simply strolled in.

'Dear God, it's you,' he said. 'They want you. You know that?'

'There seems to be a lot of police activity in town. I've heard that one of the deputies got shot. Is that true?'

'Yes, it's true. Deputy Greg Wiseman had his head blown off today at an alley behind our main shop. The police think you have something to do with it, though I don't know why.'

'I don't know why either,' said Kirsten, 'but I might know what's happening with Melissa.'

'That, I want to know,' said Martin.

'What was your relationship with Melissa?' asked Kirsten, closing the door behind her. She sat down in the chair away from the window as Martin stared at her quizzically.

'I was her editor. She came over, did articles for us. When she started going on about a big story, I told her not to bother.'

'Why? Why not have a big story? Surely that would be a coup for your paper.'

'*Kyler's Times* is not here to write the big stories. We're a local paper. It's all feel good; it's all positive spin about the town. I live here, I want to see it get better, not be dragged down into the muck of . . . well, stuff like the larger cities do.'

'Not even if something's going on?' She watched Martin turn away. 'What was she to you? Martin?'

The man slammed his hand down on the kitchen worktop

causing a cup to turn over and begin to roll. He reached for it quickly before it could fall off and set it back up.

'I was her editor. Do you know the stories that went around when she arrived? Look at the age of me. She's a child to me.'

'Why stories? What stories?'

'I left my wife for a younger woman once. I was forty, so was my wife, but the girl was twenty-seven. She was no girl; she was a woman. But my wife spun it amongst everyone, that I was just after a younger body. I wasn't. I was lonely in my relationship. I wanted someone else. It didn't work out. Now all I've got is my paper.

'In comes Melissa, she's nineteen, and yes, she has looks. She was charming; she could get under your skin, but she was a kid. You get that? A kid. I'm not a monster, but they started up the stories anyway because that's what they like, isn't it? My paper won't be like that. My paper's a proper paper.'

'Okay, say I believe you, that there was nothing going on between you. Were you close professionally?' asked Kirsten.

'She was pretty green around the edges. I gave her some tips, but in truth, she had talent. The success she made here was all her own. I was delighted to have her; she brightened up the place. Don't get me wrong, just because I'm old enough to know that I shouldn't be in a relationship with her or to try anything daft like that, having somebody so full of life, good-looking, and keen to embrace the work I'm in was really good. I loved having her about, but in a good way.

'But she came to you with a story; you didn't let her run with it.'

'There are darker things in towns, and she understood. She was working on stories that were feel-good, happy. This one, well, this one could get her into trouble. We're a small town here. People don't like it when you rock the boat too much, especially if you go around accusing them of . . .'

'Accusing them of what?' asked Kirsten when he stopped suddenly.

'Fraud,' he said. 'Fraud.' Kirsten took the backpack she had brought with her, took out the paper from inside and placed it on the table in front of Martin.

'Have you seen this before?' He shook his head but walked over and began to look through it.

'I ain't seen it. That's from her source. She said her source had written it all down.'

'So, this isn't Melissa's writing?'

'No, but this is, it's the mine. She said there was a dodgy report on the mine.'

'Howlett's Mine, do you know it?'

'Well, yes. Howlett's is to the north of the town near Kyler's Peak, the scenic point. You won't find anything out there though. Well, not unless you're a geologist or that. It'd just be an entrance to mines, deep in snow now.

'When she told you this, did you believe her?'

'I did because the kid didn't lie. That was the other thing about her; she told you the truth, but I saw the hungry look in her eye. You need to know when to hold back. You need to know when not to throw this stuff up in front of people. You need to know when it could land you with a bullet. Now, look at the deputy.'

'Do you think his death is connected to this?' asked Kirsten.

'We don't get many of our police officers shot dead in the streets,' said Martin. 'I'm struggling to remember the last time it happened. I'm not sure it ever has. This is quite shocking for this place. I know some of the bigger cities don't look twice at it, but for us it's more than a big deal. Generally, we're a happy place.'

'Who knows that she told you about her source?' asked Kirsten.

'Nobody,' said Martin suddenly, 'and keep it that way.'

'Absolutely, but I need to know more about this mine.'

'The next place she should have gone was the town hall; the records are kept in there. If they're putting Howlett's Mine up for sale—and they may have, I haven't looked—they would advertise it. It would have been a small section in one of the papers. I don't run the ads; it's taken care of by another party. I'm busy enough doing the stories. The advertisements run through the free magazine as well. They may have advertised it, may have put it out, but if there's any activity on that mine, the detail will be held in the town hall.'

'And you think she went to the town hall?'

'I told you, I saw the hunger in Melissa's eyes. I didn't want her to. I told her not to go digging but she did, and I don't want you digging too far either. They know you're here?'

'No, there was nobody out front when you got off the bus. I was on it too. I came in via the rear so the neighbours wouldn't see me arrive.'

Martin nodded, walked through to his front room turning to say to Kirsten, 'Why don't you come through in here and sit down; it's a lot more comfortable. I'll just get the curtains.'

Kirsten waited while the man prepared the room at the front. He put on a small fire which Kirsten migrated to as soon as she came in, but she noted that Martin had a grim look on his face.

'There's a car out front and somebody there, I don't recognise them. I'm wondering if you do.' Kirsten walked over to the curtains, moved them slightly to look out. There was a black car and a man with a thickset jaw. His nose looked Roman and there was a slight tan to him as well.

'No, don't know him but he's not the police.'

'What makes you say that?'

'Why would the police watch you with a plainclothes officer? You're going to know them all anyway from around the town. No, this is somebody else.'

'Who are you?' asked Martin.

'I told you before, a friend of Melissa. Her parents are keen to find out where she is.'

'No, you're not. You're not a friend in that sense. You're not just somebody who's worried about her. People like that just come in, blurt out questions. They go and ask the police how they can help to see what's going on. The police act around you as if you're some sort of threat. I'll say this for our sheriff, he's not an idiot. He knows when people are dangerous. Are you dangerous?'

'Yes, Martin, I am,' said Kirsten. 'I'm not going to tell you where I'm from or who I am because if I do that, you'll have something to tell. A secret to keep you don't want to. But understand, I'm here for Melissa. I'm here to understand what's happened to her. Outside of that, I don't want to upset anybody else. The man out front is not somebody I'm going to entertain, not somebody I'm going to make a connection with. I'll disappear out the back, and as far as you're concerned, you haven't seen me.'

'Don't worry about that,' said Martin. 'The last thing I want to tell the police is you've come to my house. They won't see that as a good thing.' Kirsten nodded, stood beside the fire again, warming up her hands momentarily and then turned towards the back door.

'Where will you go next?' asked Martin.

'Melissa went to the town hall probably. Time to follow the path.'

'You know, the longer you take to surface in front of the police, the more they'll think that you shot the deputy. Did you?'

'I haven't got a weapon with me,' said Kirsten. 'Not a gun, not a knife. Trust me when I say I didn't do harm to that deputy. Now I better get on. Keep your head down, Martin, but if you hear anything about Howlett's Mine, you can contact me, here's my number. You can tell him you had it in case you heard any news about Melissa for me; that's plausible.'

Martin nodded. Kirsten was aware he watched her all the way out the back door and into the woods. *He's afraid*, she thought, *very afraid, but it's not a direct threat. It's just generally who we're dealing with*. This was not good.

Chapter 11

Kirsten sat in her car and placed a call through her mobile, back to her own home; it took five rings before Craig picked up the call.

'Hey, how are you doing?'

'Same as ever; legs still don't work; still not there.'

'But are you okay?' asked Kirsten.

'When am I ever going to be okay? But it's all right—your babysitter came around.'

'He's not a babysitter. I just asked Seoras to pop in, seeing I wasn't about, in case you needed anything.'

'Told you I can do it myself. Have you got anything worth saying, or are you just ringing up to gloat about what you have achieved?'

'Don't, Craig,' said Kirsten. 'I get you're pissed at me being here and it not being you, but remember, you sent me; you told me to go.'

'Well, it's hardly as if I could go, was it?'

Kirsten could feel tears rolling down from her eyes as she spoke to him. He was so bitter. She still struggled to understand his anger towards her. 'I need to know about Melissa's parents; did they know anything about the story she was working on?'

'You spoke to them, didn't you?'

'Yes, but need you to check again. I need you to ferry the call through in case somebody is listening.'

'What do you mean?'

'I'm on the run, well, sort of,' said Kirsten. 'I'm keeping low, I don't want to be spotted until I'm ready to be. If I place a call to the parents, somebody might be onto that. They might look to trace back to me.'

'They could trace you from me though, couldn't they?'

'No, they can't,' said Kirsten, 'we're using a secure line. I don't care what they know; what I do care is that I know what they know. If somebody else finds out, that's fine.'

'I take it you haven't found her then,' spat Craig.

'No,' said Kirsten. 'Don't know if she's alive or not, but something's going on here.'

'When I spoke to them, I told you everything that they told me,' said Craig.

'Did they tell you anything about a mine?'

'No,' he said, 'nothing about that. Melissa was excited; she disappeared. They don't know anything.'

'Okay, all right. I'll just have to do it the other way. Anything I can do for you though?' asked Kirsten.

'Like what? Get me a new set of legs?'

'That's an option,' said Kirsten, almost choking on her words. 'I don't care about the money.'

'I don't care no more anyway,' said Craig, 'but you can call your carer off; told you I can look after myself. It's up to me to deal with this. Go sort your case.'

The phone went down, and Kirsten sniffed hard. She was worried about him; that's why she'd gone through him. She could have called the parents direct. She could have worked that somehow, but no, she'd gone to Craig, and she shouldn't have. She should have just called him and asked him how he was, but she knew the row was coming. He wasn't coping, and here she was stuck on the other side of the world, not coping with the situation either.

She sniffed, used the back of her hand to wipe her nose, and then rubbed the tears from her eyes. She was going to have to break into the town hall. Kirsten waited until midnight before driving around the town hall in the car. Inside was dark, and she wondered what sort of a security system they had. Maybe it wasn't that complicated; after all, this wasn't a big city. What of value was being held here? Nothing of great importance, not unless they were falsifying records.

After parking the car some distance away, Kirsten walked up through the snow and was thankful when it began to increase. It was almost a blizzard condition. As she arrived, and with the wind whipping up, she thought the one thing she wouldn't be was heard. Looking at the outside of the building, Kirsten was able to identify the type of security system that was being used. It was a basic motion sensor, and she located the outside control panel, opening up the system. She checked the wires, before executing a loop that indicated to the system it was still armed, but no feedback from the sensors was coming in to say anything was wrong.

Once she had completed that, with her lock pick tools, she was able to break into a service entrance and walk around the dark interior. There was no one inside, and a security guard seemed redundant. Most of the important things would be stored on files—computer records—but Martin had said that the survey records would have been held in the town hall.

Kirsten crept up the central staircase and found the local department office responsible for all the land holdings. The door was open as she walked in, and she saw a small office to one side, which must have been for the clerk, and another room beyond it with a mass of filing cabinets. They were locked at the top, but that presented no problem to Kirsten, and soon she was pulling out records here and there, trying to identify where Howlett's Mine would be in the filing system.

It wasn't easy because everything was located into geographical areas which had all been given a code, but the legend for the code was held in another part of the office. It was a good hour and a half before Kirsten was able to locate exactly where Howlett's Mine would be. As she flipped through the filing system, she eventually dragged out a small file and opened it on top of the storage facility.

'What do we have here?' she said to herself, 'Howlett's Mine, that's one hundred and fifty years ago that claim.' She scanned the document, reading how the area had been taken back under municipal control, but recently another survey had been done. She glanced through it. The survey indicated that the mine was redundant. Any further deposits of gold would have been minimal.

There was an application to sell the land, which had been signed off by the mayor. There was also a small advert that had been photocopied and placed in the file indicating that sealed bids for the land would be taken over the next few weeks, after which all parties would be required to present themselves in the town hall where the winning bidder would be the first to be offered to complete the sale. Any not arriving would have their bids discounted.

Kirsten wasn't sure if that's how things normally worked

back home. She also saw several bids documented at the rear of the file. The first one was from a Peter Germaine; his occupation was a hotelier. The amount of his bid wasn't recorded. Kirsten thought they must keep that secret or else the envelopes were sealed that the bids came in. Would it be done that way these days? Maybe there's simply some sort of computer link that they used.

She made a note of the name Peter Germaine, then looked at the next and saw a Wendy Dumas. Her occupation was as a landlady. The one following it was Orla Fontaine and she was registered as a local landowner, owner of Fontaine Hog Meats. The last registered bidder was Federico Montalbano, described as a haulier and his location was given as Italy.

Kirsten replaced the necessary paperwork, made her way back out of the office making sure that everything was left as it was, and descended the stairs to exit the building. Once outside, she rechecked the bypass line on the security system, leaving the town hall as it would have been before. Walking back to her car, she drove out of town, parking up in a forest car park by the side of the main road. When she checked her phone, it still had a mobile signal. She tore into the internet to find out about the four parties whose names she'd written down.

Peter Germaine owned hotels in many places including one in the town. It was the grander one in the centre, one that Kirsten wasn't going to pay good money for. Why? Because she was happier to be much more low-key, a traveller, not a rich tourist. The internet also said that Germaine had made a fortune in Alaska but mainly he worked down in Anchorage. It seemed bizarre to Kirsten that the man had any nominal interest in the land unless he was going to build a hotel there.

After all, it was within view of Kyler's Peak, the natural drop that gave the town its name. Kirsten wasn't convinced.

Orla Fontaine was easy to look up as well. Owner of Fontaine Hog Meats, she had a twenty-five-year history of doing well in the business. Did she need more land? Could it be useful? Or was she on the other end of the conversation saying that a false report had been submitted? She was local. Maybe because of that, she knew more than other people.

Federico Montalbano ran haulage throughout the area and through a good part of Alaska, although he had his roots in Italy and also in America's more southern states. Once again, Kirsten thought this was a crazy place for him to be buying up. After all, you wouldn't be sticking a lorry park out there, would you? He must know more.

The last party, Wendy Dumas, was much harder to track down. She was able to find several of the buildings Dumas owned as a landlady. Now, at four in the morning, Kirsten drove through the town to find them. She was surprised that at one, that lights were still on. She wondered what sort of activity was taking place. As she was out and about and believing that when she next made herself known to the police, they could keep her within their confines for a few days, she thought it best to check out Wendy Dumas straightaway. The building she had come across was a large house, old, maybe over one hundred years and had large bay windows.

Higher up, some of the windows had balconies around them. It looked like a grand house from a bygone era. Because of the number of trees around the property, it was easy for Kirsten to climb up and then lean out on the branches to bring herself closer to some of the windows. At a stretch, she managed to grab a hold of one of the balconies, haul herself up onto it, and stood beside a window with bright light shining out from it. Cautiously, she peered around the corner into the room.

The room was plush, satin sheets and a bed that looked overindulgent. There was a mirror on the ceiling as well as erotic artwork around the walls, but it was the two figures in the middle of the floor that almost made Kirsten start.

A man on his knees was handcuffed and blindfolded, wearing next to nothing. Standing over him was a woman with a whip and not a lot else. Kirsten understood the service that Wendy Dumas provided, if not by herself, at least by using others.

It took her a few minutes to jump back to the tree, climb down and get back to the car. She drove to an all-night diner, taking out her food and parking up again in the dark to eat it. She thought this a sensible precaution in case she went back to the hotel and got pulled in by the police. You never knew when you were going to eat and sometimes you just had to do it. Sitting in the car, she thought about what she had learned.

There was a blind auction coming. The bids were in and in three days' time, someone was going to win. Peter Germaine, a hotelier, was bidding on a scrap piece of land. Maybe he wanted to build something out there—it was a possibility.

Wendy Dumas seemed to have no good reason to be bidding. Surely, she could find any piece of land if she wanted to build a new brothel.

Orla Fontaine, successful business owner, so maybe she wanted to turn the land into a place for more hogs but why this place in particular?

Federico Montalbano seemed to have no good reason to even be in this contest. She wished she could see the price of the bids. After all, it was blind. So, who knew what they were? One thing that Kirsten did know was that Melissa Carson had stumbled upon something. She didn't know all the details yet, and she didn't know who was behind it, but without a shadow of a doubt, something was amiss in this town.

Chapter 12

Having gathered her thoughts, Kirsten believed that it was time to resurface. When she came back to the hotel, she could see the police were still outside despite it being six in the morning, so she returned to town, dropped her car off, and caught a bus close to the hotel. She then walked out through the snow-covered path by the river around the rear of the hotel, and located her room. Breaking in, she proceeded to take a shower and then wash her clothing in the bath, letting all the blood stains run out.

Once she was sure they were all clear, she dropped them in a cleaning bag for the hotel to wash them properly and threw in extra clothing. She then delved into her small bag, putting on a pair of black leggings, found another black T-shirt, and put on her normal leather jacket. It would be cold but her larger coat was in the wash.

She took a knife and made a few rips in the larger coat as well as in the jeans she'd just washed. She wanted to make a story up about having a fall and that's why they were being cleaned. Now, they were inside a wash bag, and she left that just outside the door of her room before making her way down towards breakfast. She acted quite nonchalantly as the service staff watched her lift several croissants, some bacon and eggs, and sit down to eat them in the middle of the restaurant.

Glancing out the window, she could see the police car, and one of the staff went out to speak to them. Soon, another police car pulled up and the sheriff marched out of it into the hotel. As Kirsten pushed her plate aside and drank some coffee, he stormed over to her.

'Where the hell have you been?'

'I've been out and about. I'm a tourist. I went out into the mountains for a bit, wanted to see things.'

'Dressed like that?' he said. 'You're full of it.'

'No, I had my coat and that on, but it got ripped. I had a fall. Why? What's up?'

'What's up? You just . . .' He suddenly went quieter and pulled a chair from one side of the table and sat down in front of her. 'You weren't anywhere, missy. You were downtown. One of my deputies is dead.'

Kirsten let a look of shock and horror come across her face, but the man was incredulous. 'Don't,' he said. 'Don't even start that. We've done some checking on you because you've got a bit of a history from what I know. You need to come for a drive with me. We're not going to talk about things here.'

'Are you taking me down the station then? Because I don't understand. I'm sorry your deputy's dead but I wasn't there.'

'Oh, you were there,' he said. 'I can't prove it, but you were there.'

'How do you know?' asked Kirsten, but the man just looked at her.

'You're coming with me; get up.'

'Do I have to? I want to finish my coffee.'

The man seethed. 'Get up or I'll haul you out of here in

handcuffs.'

Kirsten coughed politely, stood up, pushed her chair back in, and followed the sheriff out of the building. He pointed to his police car and Kirsten sat in the back while the sheriff drove her off. She was wondering why nobody else got into the car with him, and she kept her eyes focused on his hands and the gun at his side.

'Nobody else with us?'

'No,' he said. 'You and I need to have a talk. I don't know what's going on in this town, but I firmly believe you do. I told you not to mess about. I don't take it kindly when one of my deputies is dead.'

'Well, that's fair enough,' said Kirsten, 'but what's it got to do with me?'

'That's enough,' he said. 'We'll talk when we get there.' Kirsten sat back and noticed that they were heading out of town instead of down to the station. Soon they were driving up the climb towards Kyler's Peak, which she could just about make out. With the snow that was falling, last night's blizzard conditions had relented slightly but there was still a steady deposit.

The road up to Kyler's Peak was steep. The police car had snow chains and despite this, it still climbed up slowly until it arrived at what was an abandoned car park. No one would come up here in these conditions.

'Get out,' said the sheriff, and Kirsten looked at him. He took out his gun and pointed it at her. 'I said get out.' Kirsten put her hands up and slowly slid out of the car. 'Over there,' he said.

'Over there? Why?' she asked. 'I don't think there's anyone about; we could speak here.'

'I want to show you something.'

With the gun pointed in her back, Kirsten was forced to follow the path that led to the viewpoint at Kyler's Peak. Just over the railing was a huge drop down towards the town below.

'Get up on the railing,' said the sheriff. Kirsten looked at him. 'I said, get up on the railing.' Carefully, she climbed up, keeping two hands on the railing and crouching down in a squat position.

'This is Kyler's Peak, popular suicide point. It's a long fall. I don't know why you're here but see the drop behind you, and the water falling down it? We get the odd couple of accidents happen, and I think one's coming your way sharpish. The weather's closing in and that's when those accidents tend to happen.'

'Are you telling me to get out of town?' asked Kirsten.

'You catch on quick, don't you?' he said, and gave a sneer. 'You may not have killed my deputy, but you're involved and I don't want to see any more of my people getting injured.'

'Well, why don't you stick me in jail then? Lock me up in a cell if you think I'm that bad.'

'And a cell's going to hold you, is it? Oh, I've checked your records. We got friends.'

'I've got friends, too,' said Kirsten, 'and currently, I'm trying to find where their daughter is. That's all I care about; Melissa is somewhere.'

'The little trollop probably ran off,' said the sheriff. 'Happens a lot. Maybe Marty made a pass at her. That's the way I see it. Martin probably had a go. She got scared and she legged it. Maybe she liked him in the first place.'

'Maybe she knows something, found something out.'

'This is a peaceful town,' said the sheriff, 'we don't get

surprises here. You leave town. Stop digging. Stop involving yourself in our business. I'll take care of that, because if you don't stop involving yourself, accident's going to happen. That drop's a big one. You won't come back from that. This is my town and I deal with things in my way.'

Kirsten never took her eyes off the man's gun, sizing up his reactions. It wasn't the first time she'd had somebody point a gun at her. She thought about how she could get out of this. If he fired and hit her, she'd fall down the drop. She'd have to be ready to spring, better not to bring him to that point.

'You've made a really dumb move though, haven't you?' she said, and watched the man raise his eyebrows. 'You've told me this is how you'll sort it out. What's to stop me sorting it out my way then?'

'What's to stop me shooting you now?'

'Well, one, that isn't silenced. You'll get a loud ricochet all around here. I'll then fall down there and create a massive mess. You took me up here. Plenty of people saw it.'

'No, they didn't. They told me when you came back; we checked your room. There was nothing in there of note. My boy was tailing you. You know that.'

'Of course, I knew he was tailing me; that's why I lost him. He was rubbish at it as well. You shouldn't send a kid to do a job like that. I doubt you could do it better though.'

'You do understand that I'm the one holding the gun here?' asked the sheriff. 'If I wanted to . . .'

'If you had wanted to, I would be down the bottom but you're scared about that because you don't know who's going to follow. You say you know my background but you don't know who I work for now. You don't know who Melissa's connected to. That's the problem, so you want me to just disappear. In fact, you might even offer me money if you have any, but I think Melissa's still alive, so I am going to stay around here. Someone's prepared to kill, though I don't know why they've killed your deputy.'

'I don't know either.'

'Well, Sheriff, I find that a little hard to believe because either you guys are involved or maybe they shot the wrong person. Either way, I'll find out. That's the thing about these places,' said Kirsten, 'secrets and lies. This used to be a rich place, plenty of gold from the mines. Not so rich anymore.'

'Oh, this place does all right,' said the sheriff, 'but we keep things quiet. Stay out of my way—get out of here. When I find her, I'll tell you where she is, and you can go and get her. Until then, keep out of my way. Better still, get out before this storm comes in because when it does, we'll not be going anywhere, not for a few days. These storms are when things happen to people. I sure hope nothing happens to you.'

The man turned, walking back to his car. 'Are you just going to leave me here?' said Kirsten.

'That's about the long and short of it,' he said. As the words were coming from his mouth, Kirsten had dropped down into the snow and quickly and amazingly quietly, she crept behind him. Before he could flinch, she had taken the gun from his holster and was pointing it in his back.

'I think you'll find that I don't take to being threatened kindly.'

'You are quick,' he said, 'but what are you going to do? Shoot me?'

'Why?' asked Kirsten. 'You're just going to give me a lift. Get in the car.' The sheriff walked to the car, opened the driver's door, and got in. Kirsten slid into the backseat, and handed the gun over to the sheriff. 'Let's start that again,' she said, 'you can drop me in the middle of town, I've got things to do, and besides, that's where my car is.'

'Drinking again, was it?' he said. 'Somehow, I think not,' and then he turned with the pistol, pointing it again at Kirsten. 'You're very smug and arrogant handing me back the gun like that. I have a good mind just to finish you off here. Take care of the problem that way.'

'You go ahead,' said Kirsten, 'a small man like yourself couldn't do it.'

'Why not?' he asked and placed the barrel of the gun on her forehead.

'Well, I could grab it off you before you could even react, but really, I think the more preferable notion is that you can't shoot me because . . .' Kirsten opened her hand and let the bullets from the gun drop onto the backseat of the car. The sheriff gave a grin and started the car and drove back into town, cursing the snow as it fell.

When Kirsten got out, she was cold with just a leather jacket and leggings on but she felt more alive. The sheriff had threatened her, keen to get her out of town but why? Was he simply manhandling his investigation? Keen to keep anybody else off it. Did he think she was a hit woman there to solve the problem that way, or did he just not like investigators? He said he knew what she was but that didn't mean that he knew everything. Maybe the news had got through from Zante, although she thought she'd got out of there fairly clean.

The first thing to do was to go and see her four potential buyers for the mine. That's where the answer to this story would be, amongst them. She pulled out her phone, checked through addresses she'd obtained for them, and realised that

Federico Montalbano was not that far away. *Somebody Italian,* she'd thought. There was an Italian guy in the car outside Martin's house before. At least he looked that way with the skin colour and the Roman nose, but one can never be too sure.

One thing the sheriff had said was right; the weather was closing in. She could see it in the air around her. She could feel it in her bones and the app on her phone confirmed it. Three days until the bids closed, and the weather was getting worse. *Time to break this thing apart,* she thought. *Time to find out what's really going on. Time to really annoy people.*

Chapter 13

Having left the sheriff behind, Kirsten drove out to the haulage company of Federico Montalbano, the Italian haulier who had placed a bid for the mine. She was interested in knowing what his purpose was in doing so, and maybe if she went and posed as a real estate agent, she might be able to obtain that information.

If that wasn't forthcoming, she could always try and break in to find out, but at the moment she didn't want to get too close to a man who may have nothing to do with this actual situation. On the other hand, he may be knee-deep in it, in which case she wanted to tread carefully.

The haulage yard of Federico Montalbano was a rather smart set of buildings on the edge of town, and Kirsten placed a phone call, finding the company number on the internet, to see if she could get an appointment with Mr. Federico. Apparently, Mr. Federico was indisposed today, and Kirsten was advised to ring back on another day.

Kirsten couldn't wait and she saw a rather plush house at the rear of the haulage yard, its front looking away to a wooded clearing, possibly the site of the family home. It wouldn't cost anything for Kirsten to scan around and get the lie of the land with this individual.

Kirsten took the car a little down the road and parked it at a diner. She popped in to use the facilities, grabbed a takeaway cup of coffee and left it in her car, disappearing out the back of the car park. She walked knee deep in snow trying to remain on previously walked paths where the ground was more compacted, but in the end found herself having to struggle in gaining a reasonably direct route to the house.

The snow was still falling and the wind continuing to pick up. Kirsten believed that the worst weather couldn't be far off. It was all good cover though for trying to get close in. The only thing that bothered her was she was currently dressed in black with her leather jacket on and not the big padded warm coat that she had bought at the airport.

The front of the house, which Kirsten couldn't see when looking from the haulage yard, was impressive. Several pillars, large bay windows, and yet a modern look to the building caused her to feel a little bit of jealousy. Sometimes she thought it'd be better than the small flat she existed in. Craig had been a town man. It's what he would've wanted. Again, the thought about Craig brought an unwelcome feeling, one where she felt that he wasn't coping, that she needed to be back there, not here. There wasn't a lot she could do about that, so she used it to spur herself on. *Get to the bottom of this case quick and get out.*

Kirsten approached the house from the side and as far as she could see, it was all shut up. No doors open, no windows. That was unsurprising given the weather conditions. She saw the alarm system on the side. Carefully, she stole up to the side of the house looking in through the ground floor windows.

There was no one about and she wondered if Federico lived alone. The interior had the look of a man's touch, everything

95

quite simple. A number of golf trophies were on one side of a room along with a large drinks' cabinet. Through one window she saw a pool table, a large TV, and some sports memorabilia. Kirsten looked around the open-sided front porch and thought she saw a rapidly disappearing set of footprints. She approached the front door which she had thought to be previously closed but on closer inspection found it was ever so slightly open.

Standing to one side, she reached over with her hand, pushed the door open and then glanced inside. There came no movement despite a howling wind now gusting through the front door. Kirsten carefully stole in but aware that she was dropping snow from her legs and her boots onto a rather plush carpet. She glanced across, seeing a security system just inside the interior porch. As far as she could tell, the system wasn't armed.

Slowly she put some gloves on, closed the door, letting it lock behind her carefully. She walked into an elaborate hallway, and saw that many of the doors from it were open into other rooms. She knew she could glide quietly to get around the place quickly, but the windows were uncovered and the chance of being seen from the outside was increased. If there was anybody inside, they could spot you from a room before you'd even got close to it. There was nothing for it though.

Kirsten quickly swept through the ground floor. Having found nothing except an elaborate kitchen, several well-decorated but mostly unused rooms and a large gun closet, Kirsten crept upstairs. As she approached the landing, she noticed a dark stain on the carpet at the far end emanating from a room. Rather than race to it, Kirsten checked the two rooms before it, finding them both empty, guest bedrooms,

96

and then raced to where the blood was coming out by a door. It had soaked into the carpet. When she reached the open door, she understood why.

A man lay there on the floor, arms above his head but his belly slashed completely open. There was a stab wound up towards the heart. Kirsten was repulsed by the view she had. Only surgeons should see a body like that, and only if they were going to do some good with it.

A red flag was waving in Kirsten's mind and she quickly stole to the windows, took a glance outside. Was this a setup, was anyone there? She kept out of view, and she looked around the house wondering if anyone would come. No one did.

After ten minutes, Kirsten returned to the man's bedroom and began to check through his belongings. He had two pieces of weaponry in the room, both small handguns, and that, along with the armoury that was down below, gave Kirsten the impression that he was a man used to trouble. The weapons didn't look like hunting items although they may all have had licenses. This was America after all. People didn't react the same when somebody had a gun in their house. But Kirsten kept hers well hidden, more so now that she'd left the service.

Exiting the bedroom, Kirsten found a study further along the hallway and tore through the man's belongings. There was an address book on a large oak table, and she photographed every name and number in it. She noted that a lot of the numbers, names, and addresses seem to be from the far south of America and she felt very out of her depth. There was a time when she used to be able to pick up a phone, call the office, and numerous people would've checked that information for her. Nowadays, it was Craig back home, but he was in no frame of mind to do it. Dom and Carrie-Anne had gone their own way and she didn't want to bring them back into anything. Something like this she couldn't thrust on Macleod. He had to be kept out of any nefarious activity and he would've wanted to know everything about what she was trying to do.

She did have one hope though. Justin Chivers was still in the service. He'd helped her, albeit he'd been the guy who fired the rocket that had eventually led to Craig losing the bottom half of his legs. Craig had never forgiven him. Cursed his name if ever it was brought up, but Justin had been doing his best to save Craig and despite being part of the service, he had come out and he'd worked with Kirsten when she was trapped in Zante trying to save her love. He was worth a shot.

Kirsten grabbed up her phone, called through on a number and knew it would probably be monitored. She didn't care, for she was operating in the best interest of a British national. Even if the service saw Justin helping, they wouldn't bat that much of an eyelid, and he wouldn't tell her anything too significant on this line.

'This is Justin. How are you?'

'Well, not the best, to be honest.'

'Is that you or is that Craig?'

'I don't think you should speak his name. He doesn't speak yours.'

'No, everything went a little south, didn't it? Anyway, you didn't call me for a social event, and I take it you're not inviting me to your wedding. How can I help you?'

Justin was quite a maverick in some ways, someone who'd been beside Anna Hunt, Kirsten's former boss, for a long time. Someone who Anna Hunt had put a lot of faith in. Because of that, Kirsten knew he could be trusted to get the right details but also not to spill too much on an open line.

'I'm in Alaska,' she said. 'I'm hunting for a British national.'

'Hunting? You're freelancing now?'

'No,' said Kirsten. 'Been asked a favour. One of Craig's old mates—their daughter's gone missing. I'm looking to find her, bring her home. However, I think she's mixed up in something quite big. I'm in the town of Kyler's Peak.'

'Never heard of it,' said Justin.

'Five hours north of Anchorage. That's not the important bit. I'm looking at the body of a Federico Montalbano, at least I believe it's him. There's plenty of photos in this house of him and the house belongs to him, so two and two together. I've got a list of addresses as well from down south. I'd like a little bit of information about him if you can stretch to that. Like I say, it's an attempt to get a British national back.'

She heard Justin laughing on the other end of the phone. 'You know they're listening. Yes, I like that,' he said. 'It's quite funny selling the British national thing as if we don't know where you are.'

'I take it the Americans have put a request in about me then?'

'With Craig's injuries,' said Justin, 'Godfrey said that you would be quiet; you would settle down. The two of you would just live a life watching over your shoulder for the rest of it in case anything from the past came back. Anna told him, "bollocks", said you'd be out there in no time. She put money on it as well.'

'Like I say, it's a favour and if you know that's what I'm doing, you can give me a hand with this.'

'I'll do a basic search for you,' said Justin. 'Beyond that, I'm not giving you anything.'

'Okay, fair enough. You don't owe me anything.' Kirsten sent through images of the numbers she had found.

'Okay, Federico Montalbano, believed to be connected to the Bianchi family, and those numbers that you're sending through to me, they appear to be a large part of the Bianchi family.'

'The Bianchi family?' queried Kirsten.

'Mafia from down south. Italian gang. Quite into investments, run haulage sometimes to move illegal stuff about. FBI very interested in them. The service over here less so. They don't operate around the UK. I think that's about it. I hope that was of use.'

'Always. Hope you're keeping out of trouble. My best to Anna.'

'And to Godfrey, of course,' said Justin, almost cheekily.

'Godfrey can shove it up his arse,' said Kirsten and closed the phone call. Godfrey was the head of the service and Kirsten felt he had abandoned her on several occasions. He had taken in a Russian spy and killed her, which had led to the reprisal attack that caused Craig to lose his legs. Godfrey was not a word to be spoken lightly to Kirsten. If she got the chance, part of her would kill him. The other part would make him suffer greatly before doing it.

So, what did she have? Not much really. She looked round at the body lying in the bedroom, still untouched, blood continuing to slowly stain the floor. Her phone vibrated and she looked at it. A message arriving from an unknown phone. Rumours of something going down with Federico. Someone's been sent up to him; Bianchi is not happy.

Good old Justin. Kirsten knew she could trust him to gather a fuller story. What he'd sent through was classified, but he'd have done it separately, bypassed all the systems. He was good like that, and that's why they kept him in the service, because he'd be more of a threat outside of it. As she put the phone back in her pocket and wondered if there was anything more to do, Kirsten could hear cars pulling up outside.

She looked down as two large SUVs parked up and men in suits got out. They looked snappy, well-dressed, and definitely not ready for the wind and the snow that pummelled them as they stepped out.

Kirsten raced down the stairs into the rear of the house. As the men approached the front, she opened the back door, closed it, and raced off towards the haulage yard, disappearing around the perimeter and back into the woods she had come from when she had approached the house. She didn't wait to find out who the men were, but she had an idea. By the looks of it, somebody had taken out Federico, and she guessed that the Bianchis had just turned up and wouldn't be happy that their man was no more.

Chapter 14

The arrival of the Bianchis was going to drive the pace of investigation. Kirsten knew she had to start acting quicker though it was three days until the declaration of who had won Howlett's mine. If Kirsten dragged her feet, the Bianchis might start correcting any mistakes that were made. It struck her that the new buyer had to turn up on the day when they would announce who had won, and then if nobody turned up, the mine would revert back to still being owned by the local authority or maybe there would be one remaining bidder.

Could it be there was a killer on the loose? Somebody who knew the value of the mine. Then again, Kirsten reckoned, didn't all four of these people know the value? If they were putting bids in, surely they knew the value of the mine? She was struggling to work out who knew what. It was time to start meeting these people and asking them questions that put them on the spot rather than pussyfooting around.

She would have liked to have talked to Federico, but that option had been taken away. With the mob involved, Kirsten thought he must have known about the fake report. It would be something they could get into, a money spinner for them and why not? Out of the way, legitimate in one sense, even if the way that they find out about it was possibly not. She saw some pieces beginning to fall into place and she understood why Melissa would be taken out of the way if she was going to publish, but by whom? Would they silence her forever?

If it had been the Bianchis, then she could see that Melissa would not make it back. If they were coming up to sort things out and Federico was dead, somebody else must have been the main player, surely. Kirsten decided she would visit the remainder, Orla Fontaine, Wendy Dumas, and then Peter Germaine as well. One of them must have been the instigator behind this. Well, at least one. She'd have to work hard to find out who, but she didn't have time to do the background work. She wanted to see them face to face.

Orla Fontaine owned a ranch and raised hogs for slaughter. Her business was sizable according to the investigative work that Kirsten had done so far but when she saw the ranch in real life, she was more than impressed despite the fact that snow seemed to be covering everything. Underneath, there were barns, some of which were heated given the thinner amount of snow on their roofs.

She noticed a distinct lack of hogs in any of the fields and remembering that whenever she'd gone off the main tracks, she'd disappeared down to her knees and struggled to walk, Kirsten thought that would be a problem for the hogs too. After all, they were heavy beasts.

Kirsten drove up to the ranch, now early afternoon, and was told at an office that Orla Fontaine was in the main house possibly having her lunch break. As Kirsten arrived, Orla Fontaine came to the porch of a large, almost bungalow-type building and gave a wave.

'Hello there. Afraid I don't recognise you,' said Orla as Kirsten stepped out from the car. 'You're not really kitted up for out here, are you? I dare say that jacket will do well in town but you'll freeze to the death out here if you keep going about like that.'

Kirsten threw her hair back and gave a bit of a laugh. 'Sorry,' she said, 'and you're right, I'm not used to here. You can probably hear it in the accent. I'm just trying to locate a friend's daughter. Her name was Melissa Carson. She was . . .'

'The new girl who came to report, ran part of the paper. Read some of her articles. Very good, but then she disappeared. Some of the boys on the farm said that Martin had a thing with her.'

'Martin? Do you mean the newspaper reporter? The editor who was her boss.'

'Yes. Well, Martin's not had a great life. Maybe he saw a girly light. She was very attractive but thinner and taller than you. You look more like you're built to fight. Hiding some decent muscle under there, I take it.'

Kirsten kept the smile on her face, but she wondered if this woman knew about her background. She didn't normally get people recognising her as a mixed martial artist straight off. Yes, she had some muscle, but she didn't look like an out-and-out fighter. Certainly not when fully clothed. When she was down to the armless top and shorts, well, yes. What she was wearing now disguised a lot of the muscle.

'She was indeed an excellent-looking girl. I was just wondering because I saw your name mentioned at some point in a report; had she ever come out to you; had she said anything to you about what she was doing? Her family back home is very worried.'

'Come on, on up here,' said Orla. 'I got some hot chocolate on the go, put something in it as well. A wee bit of brandy, or is it whiskey you Scottish people like?'

Kirsten laughed and wondered again how much of her background the woman knew. Kirsten was born and raised in the highlands and that form of Scottish accent was not recognised as easily around the world as if she'd been from Glasgow.

Kirsten climbed a set of snowy steps up onto the porch where Orla told her to take a seat. There were a couple of wooden chairs at the end of the porch underneath the open canopy, and she had to brush off a little bit of snow before sitting down on one.

The woman had been right about the cold though. Now that she was sitting still, she could feel it, the porch blocking out what light was getting through the clouds above. And it was a harsh wind with snow falling slightly. Presently, Kirsten thought this was a lull in the storm. The morning had built up and conditions were quite bad, but since lunchtime, things had got just better. However, she felt that the air said that things were going to change again.

Orla Fontaine appeared with two cups and handed one to Orla sitting down on the chair beside her.

'I like the open air, but will be stuck in with this weather that's coming in. They sort of said this afternoon was about the last of it and we're going to get three days of getting battered. Make the most of the air while you can.' Kirsten watched the woman sit and unzip her top. *Surely, she must be cold too.*

'The report I saw that Melissa was writing was talking about a place called Howlett's Mine. Said you had some interest in it.'

'Oh, I did,' said Orla. 'Because around here, well, I've always thought maybe I could open up one of the mines and do a tourist attraction with it. But the money is awkward.'

'You didn't think about mines being worth opening for their own sake in case there's any of the gold still in them?' asked Kirsten.

'No. No, I don't. You haven't said your name, have you?'

No, I haven't, thought Kirsten. 'You never asked.' This made her think more and more that the woman knew who she was and had forgot to make it clear she didn't know who she was. 'I'm Kirsty. Kirsty Jameson. A friend of a friend knew Melissa and I was in the area, so they asked me to drop by and see if anybody knew anything. Sometimes people don't trust police forces when they're not from the same place. It's not right, but you know.'

'I understand fully,' said Orla. 'The girl, when she came to me, she asked about the mine. I told her that I'd looked into it, but the mine report had come back negative. From my point of view, it wasn't suitable to open up as a tourist attraction. There's no gold in it and really wasn't going to work for me.'

'Strange, because Melissa said that report was wrong.'

'Yes, she wittered on to me about that not being correct, but I wasn't looking to cause trouble. I don't know where these reports came from, and she didn't get it. This is a quiet place. I don't want nonsense like that, story for story's sake. Oh, I can prove this. I can prove that. Some other person said this. I sent her on her way. I run a proper business here. Hog farm.'

'I was going to ask about that. Where are they?'

'You wouldn't leave your dog out in this, would you?' said Orla. 'They're inside the barns. You can see the barns from here. Heat's on. That's why there's melting snow on top. It's quite hard at this time of year keeping them all going, but we do it. I'm doing all right.'

Kirsten took a sip of a hot chocolate, pointed to the ranch around her and the number of buildings. 'You certainly seem to be doing okay. It's massive.'

'It's really taken off. We've had to bring a lot more semis in to ship stuff out, and this is certainly a challenging time. Animals all in, storm coming in. We're going to have to batten down the hatches this afternoon and then prepare to sit it out for three days. You have to shift everything around the ranch to the right place, so if anyone's going out to the sheds, you're not having to then get feed to them. Everything is stored and ready. Get everyone to do as little as possible for the next little while. That's the key, preparation. Just popped back for a spot of lunch before heading out. I'm sorry to tell you, I'll have to ask you to hurry up with that hot chocolate.'

'All right,' said, Kirsten. 'I will do, not a problem.' Kirsten stood up and began to drink and once she had her cup finished, Orla stood and took it, clearing both away and then coming back out onto the porch.

'I'd like to offer you better news, but I have nothing I can tell you,' said Orla. 'I wish you all the best.' She put her hand out for Kirsten to shake it, but Kirsten turned away from the woman looking out from the ranch.

'Do you see the car out by the road there?'

'I do,' said Orla.

'That car has been watching here for the last fifteen minutes. Probably best if you phone the sheriff to find out what they're doing.'

'Cars stop all the time.'

'Yes, they do. They don't sit and watch you the way they are.'

'Maybe he's watching you,' said Orla.

'I doubt it. I'm just passing through. Seems to be very intent, however, on what you're doing, given what happened to the deputy recently in town. Maybe you should be cautious,' said Kirsten.

'Don't you worry about that. I have my own protection here on the hog farm. We can look after ourselves. Had animal rights protesters before, and those people do anything. Kidnapping your dogs, your puppies, whatever, hold them, telling them, treating them well. All they're doing is just taking them off you. Then they dump slogans and paint everywhere. Ruin your business. People got to eat hog; it's a major part of what the diet is up around here, throughout America. Why can't they just be proud of what we do? Don't you worry yourself about him, Kirsty. I got my eye on that guy. I'll phone up our boys to keep an eye on him too. As soon as the weather starts up, they'll clear off. '

Kirsten wondered if it was the Bianchis, but she couldn't quite see who it was in the car. In her head, she had an idea of the men who had stepped out of the two SUVs at Federico's, but she was too far away. She shook Orla's hand and walked back to the car. Kirsten wondered what she had learnt. She knew that the woman knew her, but she didn't know where from, or how. Who had told her, briefed her? Her story about Melissa speaking to her seemed okay, certainly plausible.

That was maybe the trouble, just plausible. Something where you could check and go, 'Yes, that's fine,' and move on. Rarely did things happen like that, even when people were telling the truth. Kirsten knew that from her detective days. If everybody told you the same story, everybody was lying. Stories came in from different angles.

As Kirsten drove out from the large ranch onto the main road, the person in the car ducked. They were certainly watching the ranch, as they didn't follow her. It was a different car to the SUVs that had been outside Federico's, so Kirsten had no way of knowing if it was definitely the Bianchis. Things were starting to get complicated and she needed to clarify who was doing what. One thing that bothered her, though, was the deputy being shot. Had Federico done that? Why? It was a very brash move. Had the Bianchis known about her coming over, asking questions?

Again, if it had been Kirsten they were trying to kill, that would have been a harsh move as well. Be much easier to have simply taken her somewhere, roughed her up, or scared her off. If you were going to kill her, why would you do it in the street? She reckoned the killing of the deputy was to frame her. She could see little other reason to it. Somebody was pulling strings. Kirsten needed to find out who and quick. She put her foot down and the car skidded slightly on the road before finding its groove and powered away. She was off to see Wendy Dumas before the weather closed in.

Chapter 15

The address given for Wendy Dumas was in what Kirsten could only describe as a seedier part of town, and looked much drabber than the rest of Kyler's Peak. That being said, it wouldn't have looked out of place in most towns as a fairly standard lower-class area. The housing was good enough; there wasn't a lot of drinking going on in the streets, though it was so cold, and certainly, if you passed through it, you would just think of it as a slightly poorer part of town.

Kirsten did note that the house registered to Wendy Dumas was at the far end of the estate and seemed to consist of five different houses. They were all connected by little sheltered runs and due to the fallen snow, she was unsure if there was a garden in front of each of these houses. A path, however, had been meticulously cleared so only the most recent snow was lying on it.

As she trod the path up to what seemed to be the main house, Kirsten went to grab the large knocker on the front door and thunder it so someone could hear. The wind was really picking up now that it was getting towards late in the afternoon but she still heard the cry from behind her telling her to stop. Kirsten looked around and saw the sheriff, the window rolled down in this car with a deputy beside him.

'Miss Jamieson, a word, if you please.'

Kirsten marched back to the police car, bent down so she was face-to-face with the sheriff. 'What is it?' she said. 'It is quite cold out here.'

'It's going to get colder still. The storm is coming in. I told you that you should leave town and you haven't. Now will be your last chance; you'll find the roads out of here will close. It will take them a while to clear it and with the snow that's coming, they won't try it until the snow has fallen. It may be some time before you get away. I suggest you get in your car, and you drive south towards Anchorage. Possibly even stay there for the night. It's only four hours, you could make it in reasonable time to avoid the worst of the weather.'

'Assuming the snow is coming in from the north,' said Kirsten.

'It is, so I suggest you do that. Three days, you don't want to be here for three days.'

'If my work was done, I would go,' said Kirsten.

'What work?'

'I think you know that, Sheriff. I think you know a lot more than you let on. There's not a lot of time left, so I need to get on with my business while I still can. If you don't mind, I'll do that.'

Kirsten went to turn from the car but a hand shot out grabbing her wrist. The sheriff then tried to open the door with his other hand, realised that in doing so, he now had trapped them together, joined at her wrist, but inside the window of the car. He let go looking awkward, then stepped out of the car, shut the door behind him and told the deputy to wind the window up.

'I don't take kindly to people coming in from other countries trying to run my business. Now, I've told you that I will get to the bottom of this. You need to give us time and you need to go. You'll only get in the way. There's trouble in the town at the moment. I've got deputies on edge; I've got town folk on edge. We don't see this sort of thing, so kindly get yourself out of here before I have to come down hard on you.'

'Down hard?' queried Kirsten. 'Why are you so obsessed with me? I haven't done anything. I'm merely walking around talking to people. I'm chasing up a friend's daughter because she's missing.'

'You make sure you don't do more than talk to people, but I'm still telling you, get out, and if you're going up to that door, I want to know what on earth you are doing.'

Kirsten looked at him a little strangely, but then turned and marched back up to the front door, grabbed the large knocker, and thundered on it. As the door opened, she flicked her head around and saw the sheriff watching her. The woman who had opened the door seemed to be rather underdressed. She was wearing a bra, stockings, and pants, and Kirsten went to apologise until she saw a reception desk on the far side of the room. The woman there was similarly attired. As Kirsten stepped into the room, she saw four men sitting on chairs like they were waiting at the doctor's surgery, except this was like no doctor's surgery she'd ever seen.

'Oh, that's more like it,' said one man.

'Like what?' said Kirsten.

'Oh, foreign, too. I love that one.'

'If you'll excuse me,' said Kirsten, and started to walk to the reception desk. The man, however, stood up. He was plump, balding, and Kirsten placed him probably toward his sixties. As she turned to talk to the receptionist, she was aware that the man was now coming up behind her. Something felt distinctly wrong and rather than speak to the receptionist, she stood very still, listening.

She heard the arm moving, heard the sharp intake of breath from him, and spun to catch his hand just before it would have reached in between her legs.

'Now, now, darling,' he said, 'that's not how you treat customers. I don't care if you're not in your full outfit, that'll do.'

Kirsten shook her head, let go of his hand, and turned to the receptionist.

'I said, darling . . .'

She felt the hand brush past her backside and reached down quickly from in front, catching it. Kirsten then stepped her leg over the man's arm so that she now faced him, and with her left fist she jabbed him hard in the face. In the ring, it wouldn't have been called a hard punch, a teaser to set somebody up, maybe shock them. The man fell like a ton of bricks.

'Oh, dear God,' said the receptionist and sprang round to kneel beside the man. Kirsten had the feeling she was in a comedy romp, for the outfit the receptionist was wearing was not conducive to leaping about. Kirsten looked over at the other three men who were sitting very quietly, trying to ignore her stare.

A door opened and a large woman of nearly six feet and with an enormous dress on appeared looking hard at Kirsten. Kirsten would describe her as voluptuous, if somewhat older, but the woman certainly meant business.

'Mandy, deal with Mr Tom if you would. Gentlemen, if you

excuse me, I'll see what our new arrival is playing at.'

The large woman shook her long blonde hair out behind her and Kirsten saw a face that was caked in makeup. She was an older woman and seemed to require to be done up to fit the bill of running a place like this. It was starting to dawn on Kirsten where she was.

The woman stepped forward, swept an arm behind Kirsten, and seemed to almost dance her out the door at the side. She took her through, told her to grab a seat on a sofa in the far corner, and then turned over to a cupboard. Kirsten sat down, looked up, and smiled but saw that the woman was taking a shotgun out of the cupboard.

'Whoa,' said Kirsten. 'That man reached for me. He reached for me in an area where you don't get men reaching for you. Not unless you want them to. You're lucky I just floored him. Put the gun down.'

'Look here, Missy; you're in my house and I have the rules.' The shotgun was levelled towards Kirsten.

'Put the shotgun down or I'll do something,' said Kirsten.

'You don't make the rules here,' said the woman. 'Get up.'

'I'm getting up,' said Kirsten slowly lifting her hands. 'I only came in to talk to Wendy Dumas.'

'You're talking to Madam Dumas.'

'Madam Dumas, not Mrs Dumas,' said Kirsten out loud. 'Ah. I think I'm beginning to understand. We might have had a bit of a misunderstanding here.'

'You're right; we've got a misunderstanding. Missy, you're going to misunderstand your way to apologising to that man out there. That's not how we treat our customers. You're going to go back in when he wakes up and you're going to make him happy.'

'I don't think so,' said Kirsten.

'Oh, you will. I see you've got the tools to do it.'

'I think you're not understanding me,' said Kirsten, but the woman approached closer.

'I said you're going to go in and make him happy and whatever he wants, he will get.'

Kirsten watched as the woman pushed the shotgun against the top of her chest and then started lowering it down into the middle of her cleavage.

'Like I say, whatever he wants he'll get.'

Kirsten reached up and as quick as a flash grabbed the shotgun stepping around it, driving an elbow into the stomach of the woman which sent her backwards. She tugged the gun at the same time, freeing it, cracked it open, and emptied two shells onto the floor. Kirsten took the shotgun and broke it over her knee. She wasn't quite sure if the last bit would've worked, but she caught it just right and it had looked like quite an old weapon.

'I'm not a call girl. I'm not here to work for you. I'm here to ask you some questions. Melissa Carson's missing and her parents asked me to drop in to see if anybody knew anything about it. Some of her notes said that you were making a bid on Howlett's Mine. Is that correct?' The woman wheezed in the far corner, doubled over, struggling to breathe.

'I asked you if that was correct. There's a bid deadline coming in three days. Have you put a bid in for it? Did you know anything about Howlett's Mine? Melissa said it was full of gold, but they forged the report. Is that correct?'

Kirsten watched the woman's face. She could see the flicker, the motion. Oh, she knew!

A door opened beside Kirsten and she saw a familiar face

enter. The sheriff was holding his pistol in front of him, pointing it at Kirsten.

'I told you to leave. It seems that you've assaulted one of the good folk of this town.' Kirsten turned almost casually.

'Good folk of this town—are you kidding me? He was here for a good time and who knows who with? If this is what your good folk were up to, it's no wonder you're panicking.'

'I knew you'd be trouble,' said the sheriff,' and you are. Get going.'

'Unless you want your pistol ending up like that rifle, you'll take it out of my face,' said Kirsten.

'I'm the law in this town. I say what goes and you are leaving.'

'Oh, I'll leave here,' said Kirsten, 'but I'm not leaving town, and like I said, drop the gun.'

There was a momentary standoff and Kirsten could feel it drive the coiled spring inside her waiting to see the sheriff make a move. She was close enough to him that if he did look to pull the trigger, she'd have time to duck. Time to step to one side, but she didn't need that. Other people could get called in higher up, not just a sheriff in the town. At the moment, for some reason, he was treating her with kid gloves. He was only trying to put the spooks on her, and she wondered when that would change.

There was a commotion upstairs. Kirsten could hear someone shouting, then there was a sound of somebody being hit. More shouting and Kirsten went to turn to work out what was going on.

'Don't,' said the sheriff. 'It's not your place. I'll deal with this. Don't worry. It's probably just somebody getting a bit out of hand.'

'I think he hit her harder than I hit him out there,' said Kirsten.

'I think you should go and deal with it quickly.'

'I'll get to it once you get to that door. Get moving, Kirsty.'

Kirsten put her hands up, turned, walked to the door, and opened it. Finding that it led outside, she closed it behind her but still listening, heard a momentary fractious conversation between Madam Dumas and the sheriff before he headed upstairs.

Kirsten walked back to her car, sat down, and watched the brothel entrance. After five minutes, a man was taken out handcuffed, the sheriff pulling him along. As he passed Kirsten's car, he gave her a grin and then jerked a thumb as if to tell her to clear off.

Kirsten started pondering what was going on, but the wind was beginning to howl and the snowfall had got back into full flow. It was getting late, and she needed food. After that, she would see about dropping in on Peter Germaine, but for now, her mind was chewing over how the sheriff and Wendy Dumas took things into their own hands.

Chapter 16

It was dark as Kirsten made her way back to the hotel, looking to freshen up before checking out Peter Germaine's house later that evening. In truth, she was cold, the wind now having picked up, bringing driving snow. As she reached her room, she thought she might have a shower just to get some warmth back into her body. Before she could, the telephone in the room rang.

On picking it up, she was advised there was a call for her from a Martin. Kirsten picked up the call, but almost immediately the line was cancelled. She called the receptionist who said there was nothing wrong and said the call must have been cut off from the other end. A minute later, another call was put through for her. When Kirsten went to answer, the line was there for a moment and then it went dead. Again, she called reception who advised that they didn't think there was anything wrong from their end. A third time the telephone rang, and when Kirsten picked it up, reception was on the other end.

'Miss Jameson, the person who was trying to call you has left a message. It appears that the line's dropping out every time it goes to your room, which I apologise for, but I can't explain.

We'll look into that. However, it's the newspaper editor Martin Carruthers, and he's asked could you meet him up at Kyler's Peak, although I advise against it myself; that storm's really coming in and that's not a place you want to get caught out.'

Kirsten thanked her for the advice. After putting the phone down, she made herself a quick coffee, thinking through what to do. She drove into town, stopping off at a mountain clothing shop and purchasing a coat as well as a hat. The town looked like it was empty, no wonder with everyone hunkering down because of the weather. There were ploughs out on the roads, but in truth, there was little they could do against the driving snow, and she wondered if they would bed down for the night soon.

Kirsten drove to Kyler's Peak and found the road up to it to be quite treacherous. After a few false starts on the hill, she managed to get her car all the way up to the top. When she reached the top, she saw a red car, but there was no one about. She shouted into the distance for Martin, but again, no one called back.

Kirsten looked around the car park. Then, in newly-fallen snow, she saw the faint remains of tyre tracks, a car having pulled away, and she reckoned with the snow that was falling, she could only have missed them by a matter of half an hour at best, maybe less.

She took a wander over towards the peak and saw the faint remains of footsteps being covered up by the falling snow. There were many, maybe as much as three sets of prints. As she reached the peak, she looked down into the dark. It looked like there was a shape down there. She could barely make out what she thought was a torso, legs attached to it, but it was so blurry due to the distance of the drop that it was hard to tell.

119

Kirsten started to walk to the path that would lead down to the foot of Kyler's Peak. She wasn't sure this was wise, due to how treacherous the path was becoming with not only the amount of snow falling on it, but also the wind was howling across it. The railings that normally would've protected someone walking down, were now around knee height as the snow had lifted the path up. Kristen stood for a moment thinking but decided to plough on.

As soon as she'd put her first foot on the path, she heard a gunshot. She was out of cover, exposed at the top of the peak. There were trees around but the viewing point at the top of the peak and the path that led down were clear of them as was the run to the car park. She thought the gunshot came from behind her, away from the car park and so chose this as the place to aim for. This was also because she had well-worn tracks so she wouldn't become bogged down in the snow.

Kristen drove her knees up high, running for all she was worth, until she'd reached her car, flung open the driver's door and jumped in. There had been no more shots. Quickly, she scanned out of the windscreen but was struggling due to the snow that was on it. She flicked on the wipers which cleared a large part of the snowy debris away but it was still hard to see out.

She was in a car, exposed in a car park, unable to decipher the shooter, and had no weapon to return fire. Kristen put her foot down, spun the car round and drove quickly down the road that led from Kyler's Peak back to the main highway. The back of the car slid as she went around the corners and she fought to control it as she raced back to the highway.

From the highway, the sight of Kyler's Peak was impressive, but she wondered if her car was being watched. She drove in through the town, making sure no one was following her before driving back to the hotel. She raced to her room to pick up the phone and called the paper looking for Martin. Failing that, she would drive out to Martin's house.

He had asked her to go up there. There was potentially a body at the foot of Kyler's Peak. Could it be he? As she placed the call, there was a rap on her hotel door. Kirsten put down the phone, walked quietly over to her door and used the peephole to see Martin outside. She opened the door quickly, invited him in, and closed it behind her.

'Where were you?' she asked, fixing him with a stare.

'I went to Kyler's Peak like you asked but there was no one there when I first arrived. Then I saw these guys throwing somebody off the peak.

'Didn't you call here,' she asked, 'asking me up there to join you?'

'I didn't ask you to join me. You left the request for me.'

Kristen strode across the room. 'No, I didn't,' she said. 'You phoned here twice. The line kept cutting off and then you left the message.'

'You left a message with me before the paper closed. I was in the back and you left it on my desk.'

'What happened up at Kyler's Peak when you were up there?'

'That's the thing,' said Martin. 'I went up and parked up, started wandering over towards the peak. Then I could hear a sound in the trees. I went over to take a look and as I did so another car pulled up. It wasn't the one you'd been driving, so I thought I'd stay in the trees. These three guys get out, carrying what looks like a body, threw it off the peak, then they stayed there waiting for a while. They seemed to get edgy because they thought somebody else was there, but they were not looking in my direction.

'Next thing they disappear. They must have seen my car. Maybe they reckoned it was somebody else, or they heard something. Anyway, I stayed put in case they came back. I heard another car come and I didn't recognise it, it didn't look like it had driven up from down below, but on the road that leads out to the mobile mast. So, I moved further back in the trees and hid. I'm not sure what happened to that car, but I stayed well away. Then I heard a gunshot, it was quite far back at the time. When I got back to the car park at Kyler's Peak, there was only my car there, so I drove off, came straight here.'

'You didn't see me up there then, because I left just before you by the sounds of it.'

'No,' said Martin, 'I didn't see you at all, but did you say there's a body at the bottom? It tallies with what I saw.'

'I think we need to go and look at that body,' said Kirsten. 'Can we get to the bottom of the peak without going up to the car park?'

'Can do,' said Martin, 'but we'll need to be careful.'

'We'll take my car,' said Kirsten, and showed Martin the door, following him out to her own car. The night wasn't getting any better, but Martin showed her a small road off the highway, which filtered through to the bottom of Kyler's Peak.

'Not many people know this one,' said Martin. 'There's a small substation here at the foot, rarely visited. The track's all right because of the trees that surround it. But it becomes more exposed; I don't think we'll get the car through.'

As the car rounded the bend in the road and the trees opened, Martin's prophecy became true. Kirsten parked the car up and together the two of them got out and fought their way through the snow, past a small substation and out towards the foot of

Kyler's Peak. There were plenty of trees at the foot of it, and also a large clearing. A waterfall ran down the peak, but was not in full flow at this time, being a mere trickle. Ice surrounded it and at the bottom, Kirsten reckoned there was an ice-covered small pond, broken only slightly where the trickle of water was flowing.

'You see this in the summer,' said Martin; 'there's the pond beyond it, then it's just solid ground.' Kirsten looked over where the solid ground would have been, but the snow was deep. Together they traversed over. As they got closer they could see a shape lying there. A view from above would have made the body more obvious. Here, about three inches deep into the snow, lay a body.

Martin went to grab it, but Kirsten told him to stay clear. 'Don't get fingerprints on him. Don't get anything on him. You know who it is?'

Martin sidled around and looked at the face. 'That's Peter Germaine.'

'He was looking to bid on Howlett's Mine,' said Kirsten. 'That's the story that Melissa was running, wasn't it? How much of it do you know?'

'Too much,' said Martin. 'I also heard this afternoon that Federico Montalbano was found dead at his place; that's not good. He has connections to down south. A few times I've had potential stories looking into irregularities with his haulage firm. Like I said before, I'm a local paper—I don't need the big story. I told Melissa that this is what comes.'

'I think I'll go and interview Mr Germaine at his house.'

'But he's dead,' said Martin.

'Yes, but if we go over there and ask for him, it'll show we don't know that. We also might be able to find out why he was

123

out here.'

Despite Martin's objections, Kirsten led the man away and back to the car, returning out to the main highway. Peter Germaine's house was lit up and a butler was inside. When she called at the door, Kirsten was advised that Mr Germaine was out for the evening. The butler, on seeing Martin, seemed a little bemused.

'Mr Germaine said he received a call from a reporter.'

'Really?' said Martin, 'I doubt it was one of mine.'

'That's funny, because Mr Germaine said it was someone he trusted, someone he thought of as having integrity. Let me see, he wrote down what he was going to do.' The butler walked over to the telephone and came back with a pad. 'Unfortunately, he seems to have taken it with him.'

'Would you mind if I . . .'

'What?' asked the butler.

'If I borrowed that pad for a moment as I need to make a note. Something you've just said, rather important.'

The butler nodded, handed the pad to Kirsten. 'Anyone got a pencil?' she asked. Martin produced one and then stepped up to the butler, putting an arm on his shoulder, motioning him inside the house.

'It's rather cold out there,' he said. 'So, what time did this call come in at?' The butler began to talk, but behind him, Kirsten quickly ran the pencil over the top of the pad like she was copying and etching. Having completed it, she ripped off the pad, at which point Martin turned back to her.

'Here you go,' said Kirsten, 'thank you for that, but clearly, Mr Germaine's not here, so we'll leave you in peace. Thank you for your time.'

They walked back to the car, sat down inside, and Kirsten

unfolded the piece of paper she had rubbed the pencil onto.

'Any luck?' asked Martin.

Kirsten placed the paper on the steering wheel, staring at it. 'It's faint,' she said, 'but it says, "Mine is a keeper. Report a lie."'

'So, Melissa phoned him,' said Martin. 'She must be alive then, not run off.'

'Maybe, or maybe somebody else did it. I really don't like this,' said Kirsten. 'Let's get you home and out of the way. The trouble I've got is there's a man with Italian connections down south, who has been killed in his own haulage firm. Peter Germaine's been taken somewhere and dispatched. I'm getting little cooperation from other people. I need to think this through; time to call it a night.'

Chapter 17

Kirsten sat in her t-shirt and jeans staring at the wall of the hotel room. The bed wasn't particularly comfortable to sit on, but that wasn't distracting her as her mind was completely on the situation. She was struggling to understand who was at the core of this. The hotelier Federico Montalbano had been killed, and then people from the south had turned up. Had they decided to come and clean house? Is that why people were being taken up to Kyler's Peak? Is that what had happened to Peter Germaine? There was nothing of note on the hog farmer, Orla Fontaine. Indeed, someone had been watching her.

Wendy Dumas was different. Kirsten, having gone in there, wondered if there was anything between Wendy and the sheriff. He seemed rather protective of her but was that not because he was trying to protect her business. Maybe he had connections to it or was there something else going on? Of the four people who put a bid in for Howlett's Mine, two of them were dead. One of those who was dead had a call from a reporter alleging that the report was false, which it appeared to be, or at least that's what Melissa thought. Where was she? If a reporter had called Peter Germaine, did that mean she was alive? Had it been her? Kirsten felt like she was trying to push past a brick wall to the truth.

The room was silent, and she had a coffee to her left which occasionally she would pick up and slurp. Otherwise, she sat in total silence, pondering what was going on. Kirsten closed her eyes, letting the brain churn because sometimes that's what needed to happen; that's when it came to her. She remembered Macleod saying that about her. She had a brain like his.

She thought about phoning him, then felt guilty that he was the first person she thought of phoning. Not Craig. She couldn't handle Craig at the moment, not with what was going on. He was still in that foul mood. If he was still acting that way, it would only fog her mind. She wouldn't get this case cleared and she wouldn't get home any quicker. Therefore, it was more important that she focused on what she was doing. He said he was going to learn to live with it himself. Maybe she needed to let him do that. She told Macleod to look in after all, and he must have done because Craig wasn't happy about it when she called last time.

Kirsten thought she heard a sound. It was hard to hear anything outside of the room. The wind was howling, snow was falling, but even despite this, she thought she heard something. Something had rapped the window, touched it. Had there been a crunch in the snow?

She couldn't be sure, but something had made a noise, and for her that meant she needed to know what it was. Slowly, she got off the bed, walked over to the window, and peered out from behind the curtains. People would've been lucky to have seen the movement in the curtain at all, but Kirsten saw that there was somebody outside. There was a man stalking about here and there.

She thought about going out to see him, hunting him down, but then the phone rang from reception. Kirsten walked over to it, pulled the phone down to the floor, and sat on the floor as she answered it. She remembered the old trick of making sure someone was located in a position before firing in through a blind window. When she picked the phone up, however, nothing happened except reception asked if she would come to the front desk. Kirsten answered in the affirmative, put the phone down, replaced it back on the desk, and continued to sit in a room.

Kristen flicked off the light in the room, however, then moved to one side not far from the door. She waited five minutes then she thought she could hear someone outside. They were clever. Very quiet in their movement, just not quiet enough, when they gave a light kick on the door. It didn't flinch, but then a gunshot blew the lock, and the door was kicked in. A man strode through, gun before him and Kristen grabbed his wrist, cracking it hard, causing him to drop the gun.

She turned and threw the man across the room where he crashed into the small table beside the bed. There must have been a yell from outside, for she heard a 'She's in here.' Then the window was blown out with some type of shotgun. Kristen ducked, wondering if shots would come through but a third man entered, and she disarmed him, driving a knee up into his stomach and sending his head crashing off the table the phone was sitting on.

The curtains had fallen down all the way to one side of the broken glass after the shotgun blast. She could see the man outside with the shotgun disappearing into the snowy dark. Their attack had gone wrong.

Kristen ran for the window, diving through it and rolling as she landed on the ground, the snow cushioning her fall. She saw the man making off into the woods behind the hotel and down round to the path that led towards the river. Kristen cut through past the front of the hotel and up a second path that would lead to the bridge over the river. The path she was on had been well trodden, and therefore, the snow was compacted. Where the man had gone, his route would have been deeper and more powdery snow.

Sure enough, Kirsten arrived at the river just as the man was coming along from the other path. He was looking over his shoulder as he arrived and was completely surprised to see her. More so when she stood her ground and kicked hard, knocking the shotgun from his hand before launching another kick which drove his knee to one side and sent him tumbling to the ground. She grabbed the shotgun, throwing it away. The man was able to elbow her in the face, causing her to fall backwards. He got up and then threw a kick which she blocked with crossed hands, before he ran to the river.

Back up on her feet, she dived, tapping the back of his heel, causing his two legs to kick together and send him sprawling. The bridge was icy, and he slid across and into the side of it, his head smashing against one of the wooden beams. Kirsten was right behind him, struggled with her footing and slid into him, but made sure she fell on top of him. Quickly, she took his arm around his back, followed by his other arm, and held him there.

She reached out for his belt, took it off, and tied his arms up behind his back before hauling him up by the hair, and then beginning to walk back to the hotel. As she walked back down the path, she could see the lights of the police cars and the desk clerk sobbing outside. They must have asked the woman to call Kirsten out. She could feel for her.

When Kirsten arrived with her captive and handed him to two deputies, she saw the sheriff approaching from inside the hotel. He took her by the arm, pulling her back inside and to her room.

'I'm okay, thanks,' said Kirsten.

'Really?' he said. 'Kirsty Jameson. Who are you, exactly?'

'What do you mean who am I?' The sheriff turned to two other deputies telling them to make sure no one entered the hotel. He pushed her down onto a chair and took a pair of handcuffs, snapping them on behind her back.

'What are you doing?' asked Kirsten. 'I've been attacked. I've just apprehended one of them for you. Who are these people?'

She looked around at the two men lying unconscious on the floor. She'd hit them good, incapacitating them quickly.

'You handle these sorts of people every day.' said the sheriff. 'You tell me you're just a friend visiting, passing through. You're causing trouble here, there, and everywhere. You come up to Madam Dumas's premises and start manhandling people there. It's not your job, it's mine. I told you to leave. The weather was closing in. You'll not get out now and that's a pity because If you had left, none of this would've happened. It all would've been a lot quieter. I'm afraid I'm going to have to deal with you. You have killed two men.'

'I haven't killed anyone,' said Kirsten. 'Look at them. They're still breathing, and they jumped me for a start.'

The sheriff reached inside the jacket he was wearing, and Kirsten watched him pull out a silenced weapon. Without hesitation, he shot each man in turn, twice in the head.

'Double tap to the head. Professional kill. I'm glad we got

hold of you before you ran to your mark. These guys won't matter. They're not from around here. Probably nasty pieces of work as well.'

Kirsten was feeling shocked, but things were starting to make sense now.

'Is she alive?'

'I don't know,' said the sheriff. 'But these guys here are the ones behind it all and you have caused hassle for those down south, southern Mafia. Last thing I need is them coming up here trying to sort us out. You'll do as the scapegoat. British agent came in, took them out. Reprisals will go elsewhere, not with us, but kind of you to turn up and volunteer your services.'

Kirsten thought about speaking, thought about letting out what she knew, but she decided against it. Was the sheriff behind Howlett's Mine or was he just aware of the Italians muscling in? Had the deception been done by Federico and then he was betrayed? After all, the sort of money that he would make from the mine going back down south would've kept him in good stead. Maybe the sheriff was hacked off because he hadn't got a share in it. Either way, Kirsten was in trouble.

'The problem I've got, ' said the sheriff, 'is I can't really be seen disposing of you here, can I? You'll have to go somewhere, make a break for it. Maybe you were involved with Peter Germaine. We found his body tonight and then this happens as well. Maybe we'll take you out there so you can help, tell us what went on. You'll make a break for it and we'll end up having to shoot you. You're gone. Federico's gone. The guys from the south are gone. You have the blame for it. That sounds good. My only annoyance is I can't go up there and do it myself. But when you've got the good ole boys, it don't matter.'

'Who shot your deputy?' ask Kirsten.

'What?'

'I asked, who shot your deputy? That's the bit I'm not getting. Is this for revenge for shooting him, or did somebody else? Certainly stir your boys up to defend you, wouldn't it?'

'Well, that's the trouble with these southern people, isn't it? Somebody told me Federico could handle a gun.'

Kirsten didn't believe him. Something still didn't sit right, but he grabbed her, told her to stand up and walked her out of the hotel towards a squad car. He looked over at two deputies, called them, and pushed her inside the car.

Through an open window she heard him as he said, 'Miss Jameson's offering to give us a hand with what happened to Peter Germaine. Probably best if you take her out now. When she makes a run for it, dispatch her, don't take any chances. Make sure whatever story she's told you is a good one. Don't need any of this coming back on us. This is a chance to clean it up good.'

The deputies nodded and climbed into the front seats of the car as Kirsten sat in the back. She needed a way out, but that wouldn't be easy. The rear doors of the car were locked. The sheriff then communicated to one of his men that he should roll down the window. Kirsten for a minute thought that he might put his head in, and she could at least attack him and get away, but he wasn't that stupid and kept himself at a distance.

'This is merely a form of gloating,' he said. 'Thank you for your time and you've certainly helped to clear everything up. The good thing about you when I looked you up was that your former service didn't want to know anything about you. They said you were nothing to them and just a pain. They absolutely wouldn't react to anything that was carried out against you. I asked it from a point of view of the Italians, not from myself doing this. It's good to know when someone's got no backup. It's been nice knowing you, Kirsten Stewart!' he said quietly. 'That's the trouble when you're one of those sorts of people. You get recognised too easily.'

Kirsten watched, the man grinning as the window rose between them. The car fired up and drove down the entrance to the hotel, out onto the highway and off towards Kyler's peak. Kirsten reckoned she had maybe five to ten minutes to work out how to next keep herself alive.

Chapter 18

The drive to Kyler's Peak was one that Kirsten had undertaken often recently, but never as a backseat passenger. She stared out of the window at the ever-falling snow, amazed at how it whipped round past the car. The deputy who was driving could be seen staring desperately, muttering about being unable to see in the dark. His headlights were not showing their beam but rather were dipped so that the light would not reflect so strongly from the storm outside.

Even the main highway now was becoming white. The snowploughs had probably given up for the evening, or if they hadn't, they were unable to keep up with the fall. There were banks at the side of the road to Kyler's Peak and Kirsten wondered how she was going to get out of this situation. She was dressed in a black T-shirt and jeans and was already cold from having chased down the only Italian still alive.

That's if he was still alive, of course. It'd been harder to hush him up given the fact that he was alive and well in front of everyone else at the hotel. Those in the room had been dispatched quickly, and so she reckoned that the sheriff would somehow figure out a way to get rid of the other Italian.

She tried to work the cuffs, but although they were standard issue, they were well-made, and she certainly couldn't get her wrists out. There was nothing in the backseat of the police car, nowhere she could rub them, try and free them up. She'd have to bank on the deputies being poor in their execution, coming too close, giving her a chance to kick out at them, headbutt them possibly.

It certainly wasn't a good situation. She remembered a much warmer situation out in Zante where she thought she was dead, and her former colleagues had come to her rescue. Not now. They wouldn't know about this, and part of her regretted not calling them for help. Would they have come? Possibly not. It wasn't like Craig was missing this time.

Craig was missing. That was the problem. The pair of them would've been out here had he still had his legs. They could have come together, made a good team, and there'd been no need for anybody else's help; would be watching each other's back. She cursed Justin Chivers's name for a moment and then remembered that that was highly unfair. He'd only been trying to stop Craig from being taken by the Russians. The damage and injury they'd have done to him could have been much worse than actually losing his legs, though Craig would never see it like that. No, Godfrey was the problem at the end of the day; Godfrey caused this. One day, she would come for Godfrey.

Kirsten didn't know if that was true or just something she kept in her head to make her get up every day and get on, but either way, the moment was coming close, and the car started up the road to Kyler's Peak. A couple of times the wheels spun, but the snow chains prevailed, and soon they arrived at the car park at the top of the peak.

When the deputy opened the door, Kirsten felt the cold

fly into the car, and everything about her suddenly became chilled. Her hair whipped back and forward in the wind, and she struggled to hear the deputy shouting at her to get out of the car. She slowly made her way out, and they pointed to tell her to stand in front of them and walk over towards the viewpoint at the top of the peak.

That was it. She would die here as an escapee where she was meant to be helping them. Desperately, she glanced down the side. There was no one there, no cars, nothing. What was going on? How was she to stop this? It seemed that the end was here.

'Just keep walking,' shouted the deputy. When she turned around, she saw both of them with their guns out. 'Bit further. Bit further,' they shouted it. 'Don't want to make it look like you didn't get too far before we did anything.'

She turned her head around thinking about making a run for it, but they were too close, far enough away so by the time she could reach them to do anything, they'd have shot her, but near enough to know that they wouldn't miss if she bolted. Damn it. They knew what they were doing. Maybe they'd done this before, or maybe they were doing this because one of theirs had been taken out. That bugged Kirsten. Why? Had she been the target or not?

'Just keep walking. It's over now. Just keep walking.'

Kirsten waited for the shot, her legs shaking like jelly, but she walked on still contemplating if she should make a run. A shot rang out and she waited for the impact, but none came. It took her a moment before she realised that they'd either missed her or something else had happened. Either way, she didn't hang about.

With her arms still behind her, Kirsten began to run for any tree cover she could find. As she ran, she glanced behind her and saw the two deputies taking cover as someone fired again. Kirsten ran low and reached the trees, placing herself behind one of the trunks. She looked left and right and then saw the deputies begin to come after her. They turned quickly when another shot rang out.

It struck her that whoever was shooting was either pretty useless or they weren't trying to hit the deputies. Even when they sheltered behind their car and the shots rang out, the person doing the shooting couldn't hit the car. It was strange also that when the shots rang out, yes, they were loud, but this wind was so wild it muffled them.

Kirsten knew she couldn't hang about, so she turned and began to run into the trees and down the side of the Kyler's Peak. Her mixed martial arts training came in, for there, you had to keep going. In the octagon, you couldn't stop, or they would keep pummelling you, so her energy reserves were good, and she ran hard, lifting her feet through the snow.

Several times she tripped, fell over, but rolled back up and just kept going. There was nothing else for it. Unsure where she was, she knew the one thing that wouldn't be helpful was going through a small mountain in a snowstorm. At least the trees were giving shelter, although running through them was difficult, and she felt her face being whipped every now and again by the branches. She had no arms to put up in front of her, and so at times when she saw larger branches coming, she turned sideways, crashing in with her shoulder, but that was always better than staying put, always better than having a bullet rip through you.

As she got towards the back of the landmark, the ground suddenly became steeper and she fell tumbling over and over down the slope. At one point, she pitched off a ledge, dropped about six feet before hitting the snow again and continuing to roll. Part of her thought that during summer, she might have sustained broken limbs for surely there were rocks under here. But the snow was thick and deep.

Maybe because of the wind, Kirsten couldn't hear anyone pursuing her, but she didn't risk stopping and kept walking on as she got to the end of her endurance. Soon the slope began to flatten out, and she deliberately stayed away from the direction of the main road as best as she could calculate it. There were no stars to see by, very little moonlight, and she was cold.

She could feel herself beginning to shiver. Her trousers were soaking wet, her top too. She needed heat, warmth from somewhere. As she walked, Kirsten came across a large wooden barn with a chimney sticking out of the top. There was what looked like a road approaching it, but in truth, it was so covered in snow it was barely discernible. There was also nothing else out here.

She walked over to the front door hoping to find shelter. There was a lock, but Kirsten took her elbow and smashed the glass beside it. Carefully, she put both hands in the created gap, and managed to draw the bolt back and then open the door. She'd cut herself trying to do it for her hands were cuffed behind her back, and she couldn't see a jagged piece of glass that had stuck out. She'd have to dress that at some point.

Once inside the barn, she realised why it looked so large. A large circular saw with machinery apparatus around it dominated the centre of the room, but there were also smaller saws. She walked around looking for a power switch and gave thanks that she could see with the emergency lights on, and knew there was a live supply to the building.

Rather than switch on all the lights, Kirsten went over to one of the small circular saws and was able to switch it on at the wall. Then, very carefully, she backed her handcuffed hands towards it keeping her wrists as far apart as possible, and she let the chain be cut on the circular saw. She gave a gasp of relief when she was able to swing her hands around in front of her.

When Kirsten looked around, outside, the weather seemed to be getting worse, and she was still shivering. Yes, she was in shelter, but it wasn't exactly warm. She looked around for what supplied the chimney. She saw a small wood stove.

Quickly, she took some of the wood lying around in the store, cut it up using the small circular saw. Kirsten searched through cupboards and found some firelighters and kindling, and lit a fire within the stove. It took about twenty minutes to catch fully, and she then sat in front of it for the next hour.

She had a friend, she thought. She had a friend, but who was it? It seemed strange that Martin would have a gun and be firing wildly. It seemed strange that anybody would be missing a car if they were half competent. Whoever it was hadn't called out for her to come to them—hadn't sought to give her shelter.

Kirsten looked around and saw some straw bales in the far corner. She dragged one over, placing it in front of the stove. She found a knife, cut the bale, and then she spread out the straw in front of the stove before lying down on top of it. She couldn't go back out in that storm at present. Maybe with a bit of daylight, she'd have a better chance.

Kirsten looked further around the building and found a small torch that she then used to scour the full extent of the building now that she had warmed up a little. She found a large orange coat clearly designed for being out in the cold which was highly luminous. It would do for tonight. She put it around her before attending to the fire again.

When she'd loaded the fire up, she lay down, going into the sentry sleep that she'd been trained to do. Her eyes were closed, the breathing was light, but the ears were listening. She reckoned it must have been around about six or seven when she got up. It was beginning to get light outside and that seemed the norm for her guessed hour of the morning.

She kept her large coat on and peered around at the surroundings of the barn she was in. Clearly, this was a wood-chopping station, a small holding where people would work the trees they'd harvested. It had been closed, probably more likely to be used once spring arrived. Thankfully, the power was still running and there'd been heat. Kirsten relit the fire as she sat working out what to do.

Her jeans and her top which had been so wet the night before had dried somewhat as she'd slept in the warmth, but now she took them off properly and gave them an hour drying in front of the stove. As soon as they were dry, she put them back on, wrapped herself up in the luminous coat, and looked around to see if there was any map or any way of knowing where she was. She couldn't find any, and when she looked outside, she saw that the wind was still whipping, but the snow wasn't falling as hard.

It was time to make it back to civilization. She'd need to check on Martin. Would he be safe? She'd need to get a car, some sort of transport. In this weather, there was no way she was using a bike.

In coming to Alaska, Kirsten had been determined that she wouldn't be breaking laws, she would just find out what had happened. Now, she was on the wrong end of the law, and she was sure that the sheriff wouldn't hesitate next time in putting her down without the elaborate backstory.

Part of her worried that the luminous coat she was wearing would be too much of a giveaway, but then again, she might just blend in in workman's clothes. She took a breath and stepped out into the wind again, pulling the hood of the coat up over her head. Her mobile phone was back at the hotel. Lots of her stuff was at the hotel. The little bag she'd brought with the remainder of her clothes. She wondered where they had gone now. Things had got complicated, too complicated, and there could only be a day or two left before the bids for Howlett's mine came in. It was time to bring this to a head. Time to put it to a stop, and time to find out who her special friend was.

Chapter 19

K irsten was grateful for the large and luminous coat that she'd found within the small sawmill, for the walk out to the road was a long one. On reaching, she managed to thumb down a lift from a trucker who seemed to take quite a shine to her.

'You sit up top front, darling,' he said. 'What are you doing this far out anyway? Your car get stuck?'

'Yes,' said Kirsten, 'my car got stuck.'

She had no ID on her, no way to pay anyone, and no phone, and realised she was in a lot of difficulty. While she sat up front in the trucker's cab, part of her thought about the decency of some people. Yes, the man seemed pleased to have her in the cab, and yes, part of that was maybe due to an attraction, but he was pleasant and talked about the family he had back home. For a woman out on her own, she felt very safe with the man, something that had been in short supply lately. It wasn't that she couldn't take care of herself if the man had not been; it was just that it was nice to see decent people in the world.

The trucker left Kirsten on the edge of town, giving her a couple of snack bars before he drove off again. She told him her name was Cindy, and that she was from this part of the world, although she had been born elsewhere, accounting for her accent. Anything but why she was there. She did not like lying to the man who had been so kind, but on the other hand, she didn't want the sheriff or anyone else getting a whiff of where she was now.

Kirsten decided to see Martin but first made a visit into a store in town, where she pilfered a snood and promptly covered her face with it. She didn't look out of place due to the storm that was around, and she made a note to drop a donation to charity for the theft she'd just committed. She then proceeded to a car park and stole a car, taking it over to Martin's. She would drop it back later in the day, swap it for another one, and do her best not to bash it up in the meantime.

Arriving at Martin's, she could see no one there, but still played it cautious, routing in by the wooded area towards his back door. From there she broke in and checked the entire house. Martin wasn't there, but neither had he packed any bags, by the look of it. Could he have fled, for his car wasn't there either? Kirsten was unsure and had hoped that Martin would be able to bring her up to speed on what had been the fallout from the previous night. After all, she'd been out of the loop, having to hide out last night; now that it was heading towards lunchtime, she felt hungry.

She made herself some beans and toast at Martin's, hungrily eating it before clearing up and leaving the property as she'd found it, Kirsten made the trip back to the car she had taken. Kirsten drove through the lightly falling snow and left the vehicle a few blocks from the police station.

The station wasn't the largest, and Kirsten reckoned from the outside that it maybe held three or four offices, a small section for the cells and possibly an armoury as well. Access to it wouldn't be difficult, but she had to be aware there may be cameras surrounding the property. So, she took her time, pacing around, checking the protection systems she may be up against, and ditching the large coat in a bin around the corner.

She snuck up on the station, staying away from the main camera, and focused on the car park. She was able to run adjacent to the walls and listen in at the windows before she got to the rear door. It had a security keypad on it, and required a number to enter. Kirsten stood outside, shivering, then hid behind one of the cars in the car park as she saw a deputy approach.

Spying the numbers he tapped in wasn't difficult, and after she'd given him two minutes inside, she ran up to the keypad, tapped the code, and entered. She had the snood up to her face just in case there were cameras inside as well. Not that it would be difficult to guess who she was.

She found herself in a long corridor. On the left-hand side was a door labelled stationery, while on the right was one labelled washroom. Creeping down the corridor, she found the sheriff's office on the left with a larger room on the right. As she peered in through the glass in the door, she could see the sheriff sitting behind a desk, making a call.

The other room was currently empty. She crouched down, about to sneak further up the hall, but she heard the door at the far end began to open. Kirsten doubled back, opened the stationery door, and stepped inside. It was dark, but she quickly found a switch, flicking it on briefly to see stacks of paper, pencils, and all manner of files and cabinets. She hid behind the door, wondering if anyone would open it, but there was a kerfuffle in the hallway.

'Everyone in,' said a voice. It was the sheriff and she waited until the noise had abated from the hallway. Quickly, she opened the stationery cupboard door, peeped out, and saw no one. As she crept along the hall, she could hear the noise from the room on the right. Slowly, she slid along the wall and perched herself down beside the door. From inside, she could hear the sheriff's voice.

'Kirsty Jameson, AKA Kirsten Stewart, was a former British agent and quite what she has to do with the killing of Federico Montalbano, we are not sure, but I'm convinced that she killed our friend and colleague, Deputy Greg Wesson, and for that we're going to bring her in. Be careful; she's already escaped the clutches of two of our men. She also killed several Italian mobsters. She's a lot to handle, but let's get out on the streets and let's find her. I want a perimeter search around the town as well, see if she's been in anyone's property.

'We also need to find Martin Carruthers, I believe he may be assisting her, whether that would be willingly, I don't know. Also, be on the lookout for Melissa Carson, our recent missing person. She may be involved in this, as I believe Stewart may have been hired by the family. Quite how all this works out I don't know. The sooner we bring her in, the sooner we can stop a lot of these deaths.

'Peter Germaine is also dead and we believe that may have been because of Miss Stewart as well. I want everyone out there. Becky, you can man the station, take the phone calls. Also, any Joe Public comes in, I don't want to be bothered with anything trivial. We only come off this task if we have to.'

Kirsten heard the chairs pushed back, the meeting breaking, and deputies soon to exit the door. Racing back to the stationery cupboard, she hid there for five minutes, making sure everyone had departed, and heard the sheriff close his

145

own office door after briefly popping in.

Kirsten approached the office of the sheriff, turned the handle, and found it open. She stepped inside, closed the door, then realised her mistake. She heard a cough out in the hallway. He was coming back.

Quickly she looked around. There were filing cabinets in the corner, curtains over towards the window, jackets hung up on a wall, and yet more filing cabinets on the opposite wall. He had a large desk, and it was probably the best place to hide. But not underneath where she may be seen when he sat on his chair, but instead she plonked herself quickly down behind it, tucking herself up as tight as she could.

The door opened and Kirsten braced herself in case she had to react. He'd have a gun on him, and she'd need to go for that first, incapacitate him, and get out. That was her plan if seen, but now she had to listen very carefully. The door closed and she heard footsteps, realising they were still the other end of the desk. Then they were towards the rear of the desk.

She heard the chair pull back and the sound of the sheriff collapsing into the seat. The phone was picked up and he dialled and sat back. The man breathed heavily. Was he carrying a little too much weight? Kirsten didn't know and didn't speculate further because she was trying to remain as tightly curled up as possible. She hoped that he didn't have to go for any papers. She prayed that he could just leave the room and she could work again, but she had to be careful. If he saw her, she'd have to act fast.

'Orla,' said the sheriff. 'Yes, it was a rough one last night, but more than that, lot of Italians up at the hotel. She took them out, but she's got away. A couple of my guys had her, but she's made a run for it. We've got to go out and look for her again.

146

Just be aware. She should ignore you from what you said about your previous conversation.'

'No,' he said as Kirsten heard one side of the conversation. 'I don't think it's going to be a problem. As long as the car's out there and somebody's just looking. Don't get worried. There's enough heat going on. Another bit of suspicion about an unknown person going to do us a world of good. You've got to hang on for another day after all, when you get the mine. It's just a setback. Don't worry, Orla.'

'I know, I know. It's been rough. This weather hasn't helped either, but look, I need to get out there and find her. Take her out of the picture before she throws any more problems into the mix. Guys from the south? They're not going to be a problem. We've got that under control as well.'

We've got it under control? thought Kirsten. *The sheriff and who? Who was he playing with?* He was talking to Orla like they were in a deal of some sort. How did she fit into it?

Kirsten wasn't sure, but she held her breath listening to the man talk. 'If you see anything, just let me know soon as . . . Yes, I got a bullet for this bitch. Take her down. I thought she was going to be good for us, good diversion, nice way to wrap it up. Just causing problems now.

I'm so sorry, thought Kirsten to herself. *Desperately bad to inconvenience you.*

'I doubt she'll find the paper girl, though,' said the Sheriff. 'That's not going to happen. The best thing we can do is take her out of the picture and let her take the fall for all of us. I'll see you later, though, but if you notice anything, like any trouble, you get on the blower to me. . . . Yes, we'll be celebrating in style. Don't you worry about that. I'll come over there and look after you.'

She heard him laugh, quite a horrible, dirty laugh that made her flesh crawl. She wondered exactly what the relationship was that was going on between Orla and himself. Kirsten braced herself whilst the phone was put down.

Listening carefully, she heard his stomach rumble, before he stood up, walked around the front of the desk, over to the cabinet that was just beyond Kirsten. She rolled herself quietly around the desk, shielding herself from him coming back, but as she heard the footsteps walking the other way back around from the direction he'd come, she rolled back again, keeping out of sight.

'What's the weight with these things?' she heard him say and begin to munch on something.

Soon, he grabbed his jacket and departed the police station. Kirsten stayed in the Sheriff's office for three minutes listening carefully but heard no one.

Orla was involved then, despite the other day. There'd been a car there, somebody watching. Was that the Italians, or was it Federico's Bianchi's people? Was it someone else? Who were these people the Sheriff had put down in her room? What side did they work for? Was Federico involved? Which side of the Italians was he on? Was there more than one set of Italians?

The ideas just kept flowing through her head. *Was the Sheriff coordinating all of this, and what was it about? Simply the money?* She was missing something. Something was tying this all in together, and Kirsten wasn't sure what.

Slowly, she exited the office, walked carefully up the corridor, but someone was lurking at the front part of the station. There was a woman there attending to the front desk, and everybody else seemed to have cleared out. Kirsten wondered for a moment. Could she break into the Armoury, maybe get a gun

148

for herself? After all, things were getting much more serious. But Kirsten refrained. It would give her movements away.

She made her way to the back door, exited the station, and returned to the bin where she had dumped the rather large coat, wrapping herself up in it. She walked back into town and down a rear street to find a car parked at the side. She hijacked it and drove out of town over towards Orla Fontaine's.

As she did so, she thought the snow had thickened again and the wind started to rise. Certainly, there had been a lull after the previous night where she thanked God that she had found the barn because otherwise, she would have frozen to death out there. But here she was, still without any ID or weapons to her name, and she needed to bring this case to a close. She would go to Orla Fontaine's and find out what was going on. What was that woman's part in all of this because at the moment she was struggling to see?

As she drove, Kirsten kept getting thoughts of Craig back home, but she pushed them to one side. What could she do about that anyway? She had no phone to ring anyone, probably been bagged and tagged. Macleod would look after him. You could always depend on Seoras to come through with what he'd said he'd do. She needed to focus and get this job done.

Chapter 20

The road out to Fontaine's ranch had been recently ploughed that morning, and Kirsten had no trouble negotiating the snowy roads. Even with the wind picked up and the driving snow coming at her windscreen, she felt at ease driving out. This is what she had trained for, what she was used to, reconnaissance, and also, being on the run. She always operated in an environment where you couldn't get caught, where you're always spying on people and not letting them know what you knew, and she was much more preoccupied with trying to work out what was happening.

When she drove past the homestead, she saw a car with a man inside watching the house closely. Kirsten drove her own car past and around the corner before she pulled it up onto one side, where she got out and put on her large orange coat again. Kirsten entered the homestead to the side of the barns.

It should have held the livestock that Orla Fontaine had spoken about previously. The wind was strong, but there was still the smell of animal manure and what she thought must have been pigs. There was no one around outside, and who could blame them for no one would be out in this weather unless they had to. It was milder than the wild night before but cold enough that people would think twice before taking a turn outside.

Kirsten approached the nearest barn, and, upon finding the door, opened it and stepped inside. She was greeted by the grunts of hogs inside their pens rolling around in the straw that had been provided. Kirsten didn't stay long before popping back out and moving on to the next one.

She was four barns in before she found an empty articulated lorry. The barn didn't look like it had ever housed hogs but instead was clean and neat and had large doors at the far end which would allow access for an articulated lorry. The lorry she found had a rear door which was open. Kirsten cautiously strode down the side of the barn, looking around in case anyone was about. Everything was quiet except for the howl of the wind racing over the barn's sides and roof.

Kirsten crept to the edge of the container, hauled herself up into it, and looked around. Over in one corner she could see a portable toilet, something you might stick inside a small caravan or take in the back of a car for use if you were camping. Someone had fixed it into the corner with a strip of metal. Also, inside the container were a large number of sleeping bags and blankets.

Clearly, this had been used to transport people for the container was fitted with two floors, the second floor starting about two metres in, and just over the height of Kirsten. The whole container was big enough to take two people standing upright. When she jumped and pulled herself up onto the second floor, she found more sleeping bags and blankets. Somebody was moving people.

Kirsten climbed back out of the container and stood by the wall of the barn. Who could she take this to? Orla Fontaine was moving people. Did the sheriff know about it? How did that fit into the mine situation? Where were the people going? Who were they?

Kirsten knew that certain parties would run refugees over the English Channel from France and make a good living out of it, but she didn't know who would be passing through Alaska. Was it some other sort of trafficking? Her mind leapt to the idea of exploited women, possibly children or even men? Was there a sex trade going on? She thought about Wendy Dumas. Well, there certainly was the possibility. She cast her mind back to the episode when the sheriff had thrown her out, and she remembered hearing the foreign voice.

Kirsten exited the barn and moved along to the next one. Here was a very clean barn, sterile, and inside, she found four containers, cleaned and side by side. Quickly, she went to the back, but she heard that these lorries were plugged in to some sort of mains. The dull hum of refrigeration distinct even beyond the noise of the wind outside. The rear of the lorry was shut up, and Kirsten opened it, pulled it back, and saw the pile of hog meat inside.

This was the legitimate part of the business. This is where she moved the goods that formed part of her normal fortune. Was she just moving something else alongside it, but if so, why? Her business wasn't doing that badly, was it? There were no external signs of that.

Kirsten dove under one of the containers as she heard a door begin to open. The large doors at the end were rolling back, possibly an automatic motor, and she soon saw a lorry pulling in to pick up its container. A man came in, and from her position, she thought he tagged the back of the lorry, and off it drove out of the barn and the barn door closed. The roads must have been picking up because that was meat that had disappeared.

Kirsten wondered what to do. Who could she take this to? Clearly, the sheriff wasn't to be trusted. He was in cahoots with Fontaine and maybe Dumas. Kirsten also had a very bleak picture painted against her. She could go to the FBI possibly, but why would they trust her; after all, her own government didn't trust her anymore. Was she running rogue? Also, did Melissa know anything about this trade for this was a trade that you could kill for. The mine was a lot of money potentially, but knowing about this could end up putting people in jail. Kirsten wondered if maybe she should pay a visit to Wendy Dumas's brothel.

Kirsten stepped out of the barn, happy now that the container lorry had disappeared, and everything was shut up tight again. She checked another four barns, finding hogs and hog meat, and another one with two empty containers, both of which seemed to be adjusted for human transport. One thing Kirsten didn't have with her was her phone with which to take photographs, so everything would have to be done from memory. She would need to take someone back here to prove what was happening. There was no point blowing the whistle quite yet.

Getting back to her car and departing the homestead, Kirsten drove past the man sitting in the car watching Orla Fontaine's home. She parked up some distance away, curious about who this person was. It wouldn't be easy to get close to him, and more than that, form any sort of surprise. She couldn't listen discreetly for there was little else around the car. Regardless, she gave it a wide birth and managed to hunker down in the snow watching from a distance.

153

She saw a sheriff's car arrive. Kirsten was interested to see the man's reaction as the sheriff walked up to the front of Orla's house where she greeted him like one neighbour might greet another. There was a snatch of conversation, and she saw that the man in the car had binoculars out looking at them. Soon they disappeared inside, and she watched as the man continued with his binoculars.

Kirsten decided that she wanted to know what was going on as well and proceeded to return back to her route via the barns so she could approach the house from the rear. She managed to get there without incident and then approached the house and sneaked to the back to try and listen in. She could see two figures in the kitchen and manoeuvred herself to be sitting underneath.

The wind was harsh though, and she struggled to hear any words. Briefly, she tried to peer up and over and saw the sheriff embracing Orla. Maybe they were doing this in the rear so the man at the front couldn't see. It had taken Kirsten a good five minutes to get round, and almost immediately, the sheriff was departing again.

Kirsten snuck to the side of the house and didn't want to go any further lest the guy in the car managed to see her. The last thing she needed was to be spotted in case he was a friendly looking out for Orla Fontaine. After all, she did say she had her own security.

Kirsten watched as the sheriff drove away and cursed herself for not finding out any information from what he said to Orla. Quickly, she made her way back past the barn, off to a position in the field where she was able to look at the man in the car again. He just sat there, staring, not making any phone calls or making notes. Occasionally, he'd lift a paper like he was doing a crossword or something and then put it back down again.

The man was bugging Kirsten. Everybody else had been so dynamic. The Italians had come for her. Somebody had killed Federico Montalbano. Peter Germaine had been thrown off Tyler Peak. The sheriff had chased after her, forcing her out into the wild. Martin had disappeared, and all the while, this man sat in the car watching Orla's house.

What was he? Security, FBI, some sort of hitman waiting his turn? He's very overt, thought Kirsten, *so he might be security. Either that or somebody very secure in themselves. Somebody who knows that if they're challenged, it's not going to be a problem.*

She crept back to her own car and drove back to Martin's, coming in again from the rear. It seemed a good place to have a base, especially with her being so cold, and the fact she had no money and no phone, meant that at least she could get in to cover and feed herself.

She did so, eating well, not knowing when the next meal would come. There were still no signs of Martin returning, which was bothering her now. Had somebody disposed of him? Did he know about the apparent people-trafficking going on at Fontaine's hogs? Martin hadn't always been entirely truthful with her, and maybe that was because he didn't trust her, but on the other hand, somebody did seem to be giving him the run-around as well.

Once she cleared up from eating, Kirsten searched the house for a better coat. She needed something warm but dark. The fluorescent coat wasn't doing a great job of concealing her, although she'd managed to move around okay at the homestead. Going now to the brothel, which had many more houses around it, it would be much more difficult to sneak in.

Kirsten searched through Martin's gear and found a golfing

155

jacket that was waterproof. She put it on, happy that it was black, and found some black waterproof trousers. At least they would keep her warm to some degree until she got inside. She searched again and found a bobble hat before coming downstairs and walking back to her own stolen car. Once she'd done so, she drove off towards Wendy Dumas's.

Something was going on with these lorries, something was amiss, and she believed that Wendy Dumas may know more about it. Italians, trafficked people, hog meat, and a mine of gold were all a strange concoction for such a small town, and Kirsten almost found it laughable, except for the number of bodies that seemed to be around it. She was aware that she may be walking into a firefight without a weapon. What if these Italians were from down south? When they saw things going wrong, they wouldn't hesitate to shoot. They also wouldn't hesitate to put her out of her misery if she got caught.

Kirsten looked at the windscreen with the snow consistently hitting it and then being swept away by the wipers. It was like things were flying at your eyes the whole time and you had to concentrate but also not look directly at it. She hated driving in this sort of snow, but one thing it was doing was slowing a lot of other people down.

She'd been amazed that they hadn't come round to Martin's though, so maybe he was somewhere else. Maybe they had him. Kirsten wasn't sure, but he could easily be another victim in all of this. She also wondered if she could contact those at home to pass on the story, but so far, there was no evidence. What she needed was someone here with her, someone here from authorities. Someone she could trust. Someone like that was in very short supply.

Chapter 21

Kirsten parked several streets away from Wendy Dumas's brothel, and even then, routed through the back gardens of several houses to get to where the brothel houses of Dumas were. The wind whipped up again, sending the snow into a maelstrom of white and Kirsten wondered when it would abate. It seemed to come in waves over the last few days, and in one sense it was making it harder for her to get about, but on the other hand, it was much easier to hide when people were struggling to go anywhere. They had to focus on what they were doing, not noticing things the same.

On approaching the set of houses that made up the brothel, Kirsten watched as occasionally, men would come out into the back garden to smoke a cigarette. Some were dressed rather snappily, and Kirsten wasn't sure who they were. Were they bouncers or were they clientele just popping out to take the air? The area they occupied was away from the front, obviously creating less of a scene and in the lee of the wind. What it meant for Kirsten was that the rear doors were open.

Kirsten could pop in if she was quick and once inside, she'd have to trust her instincts. She remembered the last time she entered, it was like a waiting hall, but there was definitely somebody upstairs. The foreign voice had come from there. Asian? An idea started to click in Kirsten's head. Could they fill the trucks with girls? Why? Couldn't they get enough legal working girls? Then again, people were being trafficked. Maybe prostitution was the end point. She shuddered.

Not many things turned her cold, but the thought of a life like that shook her to the core. If that was the case, she'd bring this down. But was the mine a cover for all this. How did it fit in? Once again, she still couldn't get a handle on what was really happening, but she did realise that the sheriff had defended Madame Dumas and because of that and everything else he'd done, she thought he was more than just protecting his town.

Kirsten waited until one of the men went back inside, then stole around to the side of the house. She crept across, opened the door, looked in quickly, and saw an empty hall. There was a door on her left, which she opened, and identified as a cleaning cupboard. She stepped inside, closing it behind her.

Kirsten took a deep breath and listened. There was movement up above, energetic movement, and certainly the sounds you would expect in a place like this. She tried to filter that out and listen along the hall, but she heard nothing.

Kirsten crept along the hall and found a set of stairs which she quickly climbed. Looking briefly, she saw the plush and lavish carpet from downstairs continue all the way up. On the landing, a series of doors were all closed. Kirsten crept along, then heard one open. She grabbed the door nearest to her, opened it, stepped inside and closed it behind her.

Kirsten scanned the room. In a lot of ways, it was basic for there was a bed, a table, a chair, a drinks cabinet, and on the wall were numerous pictures of a highly erotic nature. There was also a wardrobe. When she opened it, she found it empty. Yes, there were hangers, but nothing hanging in it. Clearly the room wasn't in use.

Kirsten listened at the wall on either side and realised that the other rooms were occupied. What was her plan here? She'd need to get hold of some of these girls and talk to them to find out what was happening. But Kirsten heard a rap at the door. Someone was wanting in.

'Are you ready? Because I'm coming in. The big man's in town.'

If the situation hadn't been so precarious, Kirsten would have laughed out loud. But instead, she took off her jacket and told the man she'd be ready in a moment.

'Don't keep me waiting. I get the full hour, you know?'

Kirsten tore off her jeans, threw them into the wardrobe and took off her top, standing in just her underwear. She gave out a gentle, 'Come in.' and watched as the door opened and a tall man, well over six feet in height, stepped through. He looked strong, but also very tanned. Clearly, he was appreciative of her, but then he said, 'I thought I had got the Jap. Where's the Jap?'

'I not understand,' said Kirsten, trying to put on an Eastern European accent. 'Jap?'

'The Japanese girl. I was meant to get the Japanese girl. I'm happy to have you both, but I distinctly said the Japanese girl. I've got a thing for their hair. Can you go find her?'

'She be here in minute,' said Kirsten, who walked over to the bed and lay down. 'Come,' she said. She watched the man undo the tie he was wearing, take off his jacket suit, and then flop on the bed beside her. She reached over, her hand rubbing down his shoulder, kissed him gently on the cheek before rolling him, so he now lay on his front. She straddled him and started to rub his shoulders.

'Oh, that's good. I don't usually get that sort of service. I'm liking that.'

'This is good, yes? I good at this.'

'But I want to turn over and watch,' he said, and Kirsten lifted her leg and the man turned over, and she straddled him again. She leaned forward, rubbing his shoulders, and watched as his eyes were all over.

'What name I call you?' she said.

'Whatever you want. How about big boy?'

'How about filth?' said Kirsten. She laid down a jab into the side of his neck, striking a nerve that caused the man to instantly pass out. She felt like grabbing him and throwing him out the window, but instead, she got up and looked around the room for something to restrain him with. He'd said an hour, so for an hour she wouldn't be disturbed unless the Japanese girl came in.

Kirsten started opening the drawers on a small dresser at the side. Inside were a pair of pink, furry handcuffs. Soon she had the man straddled on the bed, tied to the bedposts with a gag stuck in his mouth.

As she finished, she looked at him and wondered if the restraints had ever been used so effectively. And then she had a horrible thought that yes, they probably were. Kirsten was a very simple girl when it came to her love life, but she found herself shaking her head at some of the things she was seeing.

There came a knock at the door. Kirsten stepped just behind it. The door opened and a small Asian girl walked in. Kirsten clasped her hand over her mouth, pulled her inside, closing the door behind her.

'I'm not here to harm you. Don't panic. I'm not going to harm you.'

The girl tried to kick, and Kirsten felt her trying to scream. A bite came on Kirsten's hand, but she ignored it, holding the girl tight. 'I'm not here to hurt you.' Slowly, she forced the girl down to the ground, pinning her shoulders, knelt over her and looked into her face.

'Not here to hurt you.'

She held a finger up to her lips. The girl nodded, and then she spoke very quickly but quietly. Kirsten didn't know any Japanese, if that's what was being spoken, but she didn't know any Chinese either. She wasn't great with languages, particularly from Asia, but what she could tell was that the girl was frightened.

'Are there many of you here?' asked Kirsten. The girl shrugged her shoulders at her. 'Where did you come from? Where from?'

Again, the girl just shrugged her shoulders. Kirsten began to wonder how she should play this. One of the drawings on the wall was of a woman and a man copulating on top of the world. Kirsten helped the girl to her feet, pulled her over to that particular drawing, and pointed out the world. She then pointed to herself and pointed to Scotland, although, it was so small she doubted anyone can make out she was from anywhere except Europe. The Asian girl seemed to understand, and she pointed to what Kirsten thought was roughly Japan.

'Good,' said Kirsten. 'But how did you get here?' The girl shook her shoulders. Kirsten pointed up to Japan and pointed to the girl. Then she drew the finger across to Alaska.

The girl pointed a finger at Kirsten. She shook her head. 'No,' she said. She pointed a finger at Europe and drew it across to Alaska. Then she pointed at the girl and drew from Japan to Alaska.

'How?' said Kirsten. 'How?'

It seemed to dawn on the girl slowly when she turned and put her hands at the front of her indicating that her wrists were together, and she drew in the air. Kirsten thought she saw a truck, and wheels, and then she drew about being held and about some of the things that were done to her. Kirsten felt the anger building up inside. She wanted to turn around and start pounding into the man behind her, driving her fists through him, but at the current time, that would achieve nothing except calling attention to herself. If she was going to bring this down, she'd have to bring it down properly. Although at the moment, she wasn't sure how that was going to be done.

The Asian girl looked over at the man on the bed and suddenly she became very frightened. She pointed at him, then to herself and indicated a line across her throat. *Of course,* thought Kirsten, *if he wakes up and she's okay, likelihood is he'd kill her or somebody will get rid of her.*

Kirsten searched for some method of restraint and ended up removing some whips from a drawer. She opened the wardrobe and pointed to the girl to go inside and once there, she tied her up, gagging her as well. She was going to do it gently, but she needed to do it in a fashion that they thought that the girl had been taken captive as well. The sad eyes of the woman seemed to say she understood that Kirsten wasn't happy with what she was doing.

She thought about the time, reckoning she had possibly forty minutes and then she needed to be out of there. They rented the room by the hour with the girl. Maybe Madam Dumas would come looking after an hour but she had no cause for concern at the moment. Kirsten decided she needed to investigate further but she stayed in her underwear, opened the door and walked out onto the landing.

Carefully she made her way down, opened one of the doors beside her, and looked in. A man on top of the bed, and on top of a woman, stopped, turned around and swore something in a foreign language. After a quick glance, he turned back and continued with what he was doing. Kirsten closed the door.

Was he one of the Italians? She plodded onto the next door, opened it quietly and saw a man who looked Canadian strapped to the bed with a woman close by wearing an outfit that clearly wasn't designed for the cold.

'Sorry. Wrong room,' said Kirsten quickly.

The girl said something back in a language Kirsten didn't understand and then, 'Thank you.'

Kirsten checked six rooms and discovered all the girls inside were Orientals. She couldn't remember there being that many Asian women in town. To have such a concentration seemed strange unless they were being trafficked in. Knowing her hour was nearly up, she returned to the room, dressed, knelt in front of the girl and rubbed her hand down her face.

'I will come get you. I will end this. Until then…' She put her finger up to her lips. The girl nodded, but how much of what Kirsten said she understood she wasn't sure. Maybe just the bit about keeping quiet.

Kirsten stole back outside the brothel which wasn't that difficult considering the fact that most people disappeared inside a room and didn't come back out for an hour She avoided the front entrance but once back outside, she scouted around and watched the place for just over an hour. She saw the angry Italian leaving, Madam Dumas with him and she had a worried look on her face.

That was the other problem. Maybe everything would go to ground now. The operation seemed so big though, she doubted it. They would probably guess it was her especially if the Italian gave them a description.

Kirsten spat into the snow. She was going to end this. Even if she couldn't find Melissa, she would end this and then a thought struck her. They couldn't have brought Melissa into this, could they? Would they just have killed her? Kirsten returned to her car and as she drove away from the brothel she thought to herself about how to do this, how to bring down what was happening.

The brothel would be a hard target unless she could get the FBI involved. Should she just ring them? How would that look? She was up against a sheriff. She had no evidence, and she would try to get the FBI to jump in and do a sting. What? Just raid a place on her word. It wasn't like she was a British agent anymore. She was out in the cold and certainly didn't have much standing with her former colleagues. If they put a call through, she was sure Godfrey would deny her. She would need to gain some evidence.

Kirsten headed back towards Orla Fontaine's because that's where most of the evidence and the trucks that were doing the movement were positioned.

Chapter 22

Kirsten thought that the weather couldn't have gotten worse than that night when she had to run from Kyler's Peak down to the small sawmill barn. This evening was giving it a go. The windscreen wipers were on full, throwing the snow off her windscreen almost as soon as it arrived. She was still peering forward.

Darkness had now settled on the day. It was one of those times when you really shouldn't have been out unless you needed to be. As she drove past Orla Fontaine's, she saw a familiar car sitting out front. As she passed it, she caught a glimpse of the man inside.

He was wearing a suit jacket and tie, and Kirsten pulled over a little further up the road. As she sat in the car, looking at him in the rear-view mirror, she wondered just who he was. He was extremely overt, and she thought about it, for clearly the watcher was a man who wasn't worried. He either was law enforcement, or he was their so-obvious guard. Maybe she should approach him and find out which. The last thing she wanted to do was to be running out into a world of trouble because the guard had spotted what was going on.

She thought about getting out of the car until the man

stepped out himself, went to his boot and pull on a large parka. He was in smart black shoes, long black trousers, and had a tall frame, but in truth didn't look like there was much beef on him. He also wore glasses that he occasionally reached up to and wiped in the driving snow. A hat was put on his head and he fought his way across the road, up the driveway to Orla Fontaine's house.

No one came to the porch this time, and Kirsten watched him ring the doorbell. The door opened and she thought for a moment that he'd said something. She couldn't see all of Fontaine's face, but she could tell from the figure it was she. Soon they disappeared inside the house. Kirsten sat back in the car seat pondering. That looked like an official call; that looked like somebody saying, 'This is me. I need a word.'

Kirsten decided she would be playing a waiting game because she wanted to get hold of one of the trucks, and when it moved, she would stop it. Hopefully, somewhere very public, break open the back and let all the girls escape in front of a viewing crowd who would then call it in. It would be hard for anyone to disguise that, but that would take time.

Would they move them all on that day, or at another time? She'd ruffled their feathers in the brothel certainly, by leaving the Italian tied-up, but it might not be enough to cause them to move on the girls. With the weather closed in as well, it was more unlikely. The plan of stopping the mine auction had gone from her head, for this was much more important.

As Kirsten continued to sit and watch the house, she saw the sheriff's car pull up and then saw the sheriff get out. He came to the door, Orla Fontaine stepped out, waved him in and then looked around. The sheriff was then sent back out, and his car was taken around the back of the house before he returned to the front and entered. The hairs on Kirsten's neck stood up. Why, if there was someone official, would the sheriff hide his car? What did Orla Fontaine have in mind? What did she know? Who was the man who had gone in?

Too many things seemed wrong to Kirsten, so she stepped out of the car, closed the door, and ran round into the forest beyond the house. From there, she approached it out of view of the window, but knowing that she was never truly in cover, and ran as hard as she could to the wall of the house. Slowly, she crept around the back. Once there, she saw a group of men arriving. They looked local, possibly workers from the hog farm, but each of them was a big, strapping lad.

Kirsten held her cover and watched them shooed into the house by Orla Fontaine. It looked like a heavy squad, and she got that desperate feeling about the person who had been in the car outside. When the sheriff arrived, she thought that might be okay. After all, he could be coming across to help smooth over relations, take whatever official it was away from the farm.

But then the car was hidden and now a heavy squad was being brought into the house. It didn't look good. Kirsten also was not armed. She couldn't just simply walk in, hold a gun up, threaten to shoot everyone and bring the man out before then interrogating him and finding out just who exactly he was. Instead, she could easily end up in a gunfight without the stopping power required.

Quickly, she approached the back door, tried the handle and found it to be open and slipped inside. She was glad for that, for the cold outside was brutal, and she could feel the heat of the house as soon as she stepped in. She saw where snow had thawed as men had walked across the kitchen and she followed the trail into a hallway where only one door was closed. She could hear shouting inside.

'He's got a badge,' she could hear Orla Fontaine say. 'Damn it, Kyle, he's got a badge. Did you know they'd been watching here? How long have you been outside?"

There came a loud thwack, as somebody must have been smacking the man about.

'Answer the woman.' Kirsten heard the sheriff's voice. He was angry. Almost wild.

'Damn it, Kyle, we'll need to shift them, we'll need to get them going. Tony, get back out there. Get things on the move.'

Kirsten ducked out of the hallway into one of the open rooms as the door opened and someone called Tony left. She counted in her head, the sheriff, three heavies, Orla Fontaine, plus whoever the stranger was.

'Best dispose of him,' said Orla. 'If we do anything else with him, he'll tell about this. He must be onto something to have been watching for that long, best to dispose of him. Do they know you're here?'

There came a silence followed by another thwack. The man must have been hit again. 'Stop this, Kyle,' said Orla. 'Give me a gun. I'll shoot him now.'

Kirsten didn't hesitate, stepped into the hallway, and opened the door behind which she would find the scene. Her eyes clocked the FBI man kneeling on the floor, hands behind his back. She saw Ola Fontaine taking the gun from the sheriff's holster and pointing it at the man. The sheriff stood beside her, surrounded by the three heavies.

Kirsten's first action was to run forward and kick Orla Fontaine hard in the gut, knocking her across the room. She then lifted her right elbow, driving it up into the sheriff, catching him on the nose, causing him to fall to the floor. The element of surprise was almost gone as the heavies reached in for her. She now drove her other elbow up into the stomach of another one, but one grabbed her, arm around her throat, dragging her backwards. She lifted herself up and put two feet into another one approaching her who crashed back across the room.

The FBI man clearly had hands tied behind his back, but he managed to stand up just as Orla Fontaine was recovering herself, gun still in her hand. Kirsten saw her raise the pistol to shoot at her, threw her feet back to the ground and spun the man holding onto her neck as hard as she could. His arms loosed off her. He came back spinning away from her, and caught the bullet that Orla Fontaine fired. Kirsten hit the floor long before it had gone through the man and hit the wall behind her

Orla Fontaine was in shock, realising she'd shot the wrong person, but as Kirsten raced towards her, she saw the gun being raised again and quickly she swiped her foot across, knocking the gun from Orla's hand. She caught a punch from the sheriff right on the jaw. She rocked back as he came in with some more, but Kirsten had been a mixed martial arts fighter, and she'd taken punches a plenty, and she used the force he'd hit her with to sidestep and drive a left hand into his jaw, causing him to spin.

'Get out,' shouted the bound man as he ran from the room as quickly as he could. Kirsten understood what a good idea it was and delivered another kick to Orla Fontaine, turned and found her path blocked by the two heavies. The first reached for her, and she jumped, grabbing his head and driving a knee straight into his face. As she landed the other one hit her in the back, but she delivered an elbow up to his head that caught him off guard and spun him.

'Get the gun, Kyle. Shoot the bitch.'

Kirsten didn't wait to see if Kyle could reach the gun, but tore out of the room, through the kitchen, and out into the snow where the FBI man was running. The wind whipped at them, the snow falling hard, and Kirsten had to lift her knees and drive as she ran across out towards the barns. She put her arm around the man's waist as he ran pushing him on as they stumbled through the ever-increasing snow.

Kirsten heard a gunshot behind her but thought it must have been wild. When she flicked her head around, they'd managed to put a good hundred yards on the pursuing sheriff.

'Who are you?' asked Kirsten.

'Jim Bernstein, FBI,' he said. 'Thank you.'

'Don't thank me yet,' said Kirsten. 'We're not out of it. Quick, into the barn.'

She flung open the door and expected to see hogs inside. There were, but, there was also a man holding a mobile phone. As Kristen entered, he shouted over to two more men and suddenly Kirsten was facing the three of them.

'I'll try and take one out for you,' said Jim.

'No guns,' said Kirsten, happily. 'Just give me a minute.'

The farm hands approached but Kirsten didn't wait for them to encircle her. Instead, she ran at the first one, ducked left as he swung a punch before catching him in the mid-rift and then with an elbow to the head. The next one she caught with her leg before he reached her, driving it up into his stomach and causing him to fold over. She then brought that leg back down on top of his head flooring him immediately.

The next had grabbed hold of her jacket but she spun and

flicked him over her hip causing him to land hard on the ground. She then drove her foot down into his jaw knocking him out instantly.

'Who the hell are you?' asked Jim suddenly. Kirsten looked around and saw a knife up in the office, got a hold of it and cut the bonds on Jim's hands.

'Kirsten Stewart. Former British Secret Service. I'm here looking into a missing girl, Melissa Carson.'

'I'm here chasing human trafficking,' said Jim.

'Well, it's here. They've got trucks along from here. Come on, down another couple and you'll see the evidence. You need to call your people in.'

'I need a phone,' said Jim.

'Quick. Let me show you the evidence before they get here with their guns.'

Kirsten led Jim to the front of the barn, out the door and across to two barns down. She opened the doors expecting to see a truck. There were none.

'Bastards,' said Kirsten. 'They've moved.' She ran down to the next barn and it was empty.

'They didn't come after us,' she said. 'Jim, they must be clearing up. They've got girls down in a brothel in town. Quick, we need to go.'

'Let's take my car. I've got a few weapons in there,' he said. Together the two raced out through the snow.

'How long have you been here, Jim?' asked Kirsten as he tore off, wipers sweeping as hard as they could.

'Been up less than a week. A lot of Italians coming up here. We believe there's some sort of turf war going on. Didn't realise the sheriff was involved. But I heard a rumour about the Fontaine woman and I've been sitting, watching for a long

171

time. Watched you as well but never knew who you were. Fired a gunshot up at Kyler's Peak to keep the Italians off your back. I take it you killed them in the hotel room?'

'Sheriff put them down. I knocked them out. I came in here to kill no one. I've no jurisdiction, Jim. I came for Melissa Carson.'

'Who is this Melissa Carson you're talking about?' asked Jim.

'She was a newspaper reporter. Came over from Britain, working as the junior but she found a scoop. She found out that a local mine was being sold. It still had gold in it but somebody falsified the report. Federico Montalbano was involved. Peter Germaine, who is dead, as well. Orla Fontaine and also Wendy Dumas.'

'Who is Wendy Dumas?'

'Brothel owner. They're all in cahoots.'

'Well, Fontaine's in league with the sheriff. I know that. He kept coming round of an evening. I think the two of them have something going on beyond just the trafficking.'

'That makes sense, but Melissa is still missing. She was going to expose the mine. I guess that would have exposed everything else eventually. Would have brought you guys in.'

Jim pressed a button on the car dash activating an in-car phone. 'They took my real one but there's one linked into the car here as well.'

Kirsten sat back as Jim began to call in reinforcements. 'I have them on their way. With the weather and the trouble on the roads that they're going to take a little while to get there.'

'That's one thing in our favour,' said Kirsten.

'How's that?' said Jim.

'If your guys can't get in, those trucks can't get out. They can't shift the girls. They're our evidence.'

'Exactly,' said Jim, 'and if they can't get them out, they'll dispose of them.'

Chapter 23

Jim Bernstein did not hold back on the gas as the car tore through the centre of town and out towards the Dumas brothel. Located in a fairly normal neighbourhood, Kirsten saw the occasional struggling person at their door, running out to their car and back but very little else as everyone was tucked up inside. She wasn't sure if the shops were open at this time, but as they drew closer to the brothel, they saw outside a large articulated lorry.

'That's one of them. That's one of the modified lorries. They must be trying to ship them out, get them away before we get there.'

'We need to be careful. They could be running scared now, liable to take shots without asking,' said Jim.

'I'm unarmed,' said Kirsten.

Jim looked at her, 'Is that a problem? I'm loath to hand you a weapon. I know you came in and saved my life, but I'm still not sure exactly where you stand. You know the business. There's only a certain level of trust I can give you.'

'Probably best if I don't,' said Kirsten. 'If I end up taking somebody out, they'll be long drawn-out inquiries, questions asked. I could incapacitate someone with my fists anyway.'

'But don't worry, you'll have plenty of backup from me,' said Jim. He tore out of the car, opened the boot, and took a gun out. Kirsten caught a glimpse at the man's overall shape as he stood at the rear of the car. He was thin and possibly heading towards his fifties. She wasn't quite sure just how useful he'd be in a fight.

'Why did they send you down, Jim?'

'Long hunch. They weren't going to follow it through, but I kind of insisted, so they sent me on my own.'

He took one pistol, put it in his holster, and another he slipped into the back of his trousers. Together they approached the house. Skirting first across to the articulated lorry, Kirsten reached the rear, pulled open the doors, and suddenly scantily clad Asian women were climbing out, shivering cold.

'Put them back in,' said Jim. 'If gunfire starts here, we'll be in trouble.'

'And if we get trapped in there, they'll just drive off with them,' said Kirsten.

Jim turned and fired a shot into each of the tires of the lorry. The girls screamed, but Kirsten ushered them back into the lorry. When they saw Jim standing with his weapon, they soon beat a hasty retreat inside. Kirsten locked the lorry up from the outside.

'Come on, into the house,' he said. 'But you keep behind me.'

'You take the front then,' she said. 'I'm unarmed, so there's no point me working off you. I'll go in through the back.'

Jim nodded and approached the house and Kirsten watched him open the door before she ran to the rear. As she pulled open the rear door, she heard gunfire from the front and strode into the hallway she'd gone into previously. Several houses were interconnected, and she knew they'd have to work through each one trying to find any more of the missing girls.

Kirsten ran down the hall to see the far end open and a man in a suave suit begin to run down it. As he saw her, he reached inside his jacket, and she knew he was going for his pistol. Kirsten sped up, flung herself, hitting him in his midriff with her shoulder, driving back into the ground. She reacted quickly getting up and hit him hard across the face several times, knocking him out cold.

She reached inside, grabbed his pistol, opened the room, and flung it inside. As she stood up, she saw another man start to climb the stairs across from her.

'No, you don't,' she said and then saw him tumble down having been shot in the back. Jim was coming through from the front now. 'It's me,' said Kirsten. 'These run through, so you've got another two houses to clear. I'll go upstairs if you want, make sure that's secure, and follow you.'

Jim nodded, and Kirsten tore up the stairs. As she reached the top, she saw a couple of screaming women running backwards and forwards in dressing gowns and their underwear. She ignored them, ran past the door, and then suddenly felt herself being grabbed from behind. Without looking, she spun an elbow up at head height and caught a man clean on the chin, dropping him to the floor.

Another man came out of the door she'd just passed and she punched him hard. 'Madam Dumas,' she shouted at the girls. 'Madame Dumas.' They were running here and there, scared, but then she saw a face that she recognised. It was the Asian girl who she'd had to tie up and leave in the wardrobe. She had a large bruise across her chin and Kirsten felt slightly guilty.

'Madam Dumas,' she shouted in the girl's face. The girl pointed and Kirsten thought she was pointing down the hall and went to run, but the girl stopped her. She pointed again in the same direction. Kirsten understood she meant the next house along. She turned and pointed down to the men.

'Any more?'

The girl shook her head. Kirsten descended the stairs two at a time into the hallway down below and turned to run after Jim. She cleared the first house, went through the small walkway into the second, and heard a firefight going on. Quickly, she high-tailed back out, turned, and ran to the front of the house, entering from that door. As she entered the reception area, she saw one man behind the desk popping out to fire at someone.

Kirsten sprinted forward, dived over the top of the desk, taking the man down. She managed to get a hand on his wrist and slapped it several times so the pistol fell out. He caught her with a butt to the head, which momentarily reeled her backwards, and then he pressed down on top of her. The man's weight was considerable, but Kirsten managed to bend around and placed her leg underneath his chin. Her other leg was able to tighten in and form a lock and she squeezed hard. She could feel the man go limp over the next thirty seconds, and by the time she'd released herself from him, she could see he was barely breathing, out cold. She popped her head up over the reception area and ducked quickly as she heard a shot coming.

'It's me, Jim. I've taken him out.'

'Two more in the hallway,' he shouted. 'I think Dumas is in the far room.'

'Keep them pinned,' said Kirsten.

She thought about jumping over a desk, through the door, into the hallway to cause some surprise, but with weapons trained everywhere and her not carrying one, she decided instead to pick up one of the chairs and take it outside. She counted a number of rooms down, realised she was close to the end of the house, and hit the window as hard as she could with the chair.

It took three blows before it shattered and Kirsten threw it down and leapt into the room. There was no one there, but as she picked herself up and ran for the door, she saw it open. A man stood there with a gun, and she stepped to one side as it fired. A second shot went off before she reached the wrist, twisted it hard, and she heard him crying out. He was only half in the door, so as the gun fell, with her other hand she grabbed the door and slammed it into him four times. His face became a bloody mess and he dropped to the ground.

'One down,' shouted Kirsten. She heard a gunshot. Somebody cried out.

'And that's two,' said Jim.

Kirsten peeked out into the hallway and the door opposite her opened. She saw the face of a scared Wendy Dumas and she ran over, grabbing hold of the woman and driving her back into the room. As she did so, she realised there was a man in there with her and she stopped, spun on one leg, and delivered a kick to his midriff that caused him to double over. As he bent down, she kicked again at his head twice. When she saw blood coming and the man lying motionless on the ground, she put an arm around Dumas, holding her in a tight choke.

'Tell them to stand down.'

'I can't. They're not my people. The sheriff put them here. They're Italians from the south. They don't answer to me.'

'How many more of them then?' asked Kirsten.

'I don't know. How many have you shot?'

Kirsten drove the woman into a seat and then turned and

took the belt off the man lying unconscious. She tied the woman's wrists tight to the chair, told her not to move or she would knock her out. Quickly, Kirsten made her way back to the hallway, glancing out the door in front of her to see a man peering out of another door and firing his gun down the corridor. Kirsten waited until he ducked back in and then popped her head out fully, waving down the corridor, hoping that Jim would see her.

She didn't want to tell him to cease fire and give away exactly where she was. She waited until the man in the room before her popped out again, fired a shot down the hallway. She grabbed him from behind, dragging him out of the room, waiting to see if anyone else would appear. As she held him tight, her arm gripped around him while he thrashed and struggled, the gun fell from his grasp.

His colleague came out of the room and fell, caught by a bullet to the temple from Jim. The man Kirsten held soon succumbed to the pressure she put on his neck and passed out. She left him on the floor and saw Jim walking up the corridor. He checked in every room before arriving at her.

'I think that's it,' he said. 'I think we've got them all.'

'Madam Dumas is in there. Better tie these guys up first.'

Quickly, they went through their belts, tied their arms up, and dragged them all into a room, closing the door behind them. They could still view it from the room Madam Dumas was in and Kirsten wondered when they would get backup. Meanwhile, Jim was taking hold of Dumas.

'Is that all the girls out there? Where's the rest of them?'

'They're on the road, okay? They're on the road. Kyle said it was best to get them on the road. They could hide the truck somewhere. They were going to move everything. It all went to rat shit because of her, because of that reporter as well.'

'Where's Melissa?' asked Kirsten.

'Kyle took her. It was time to get rid of her and the mayor's girl.'

'The what?'

'The mayor's girl.'

'Hang on a minute,' said Jim, 'Tell me what exactly what's going on.'

'It was Kyle's idea, the sheriff. He was going to traffic the girls up here because of Howlett's Mine. The mayor found out that it had some serious money in it, but we had to auction it off. Somebody had to bid for it so Kyle decided they would hush it up. The thing is the mayor's got an illegitimate daughter. Well, Kyle went and found her, brought her here. She's missing as well. He held her and the mayor put up the mine for sale. The idea was that Orla would bid, but then things got complicated, so I put a bid in as well, just in case anything happened to Orla. If you're dead, you can't win.'

'But what's all this then?' said Kirsten.

'That's the thing. With the mine, there was going to be more gold and they were going to open it up. The place would be buzzing again, people coming in. We would open all the other mines as well. We were going to run the town as an affluent place once more.

'The Italian mob had got word of it. Kyle was in cahoots with them, said they were going to run brothel houses up here as well. This was going to be a place to come to, serious money. They started moving in the Asian girls; the Italians down south—they were the ones bringing them in. Kyle and I were just keeping them to one side for the minute, holding them here until the thing took off properly. It'd be a steady stream of money heading south. Kyle and I would get wealthy. Orla would have the gold mines, set up as the legitimate holder.

'Problem was, that reporter girl, she found out. The mayor's secretary leaked it. She's been on extended vacation, but she was meeting up with that Melissa. Melissa's seen it, and that's why they had to grab her, but Jim's decided to close off any evidence from that. He's gone to put an end to her. He's going to toss her off Kyler's Peak. Same been done to Germaine.'

'What did Germaine have to do with it? Or Federico Montalbano?'

'Montalbano was part of their connection. He was up here overseeing it. He ran the holdings firm that was bringing the girls in. Then other Italians got wind of it. They weren't happy with it. They came to take over. That's the two Kyle put down in the hotel. He was going to blame all that on this one, and then everything would've been smoothed over, but instead, it's all gone to rat. We had it set up perfect. Legitimate gold mine running over the top of what you wanted for your pleasure. We all would've been rich until that stupid reporter stuck her nose in. We would have paid off the mayor afterwards as well. Wouldn't have been a problem.'

'But Melissa, she's up at Kyler's Peak? When did he go?' asked Kirsten.

'About ten minutes before you arrived, but he had to pick up the mayor's daughter as well. She's held elsewhere.'

'We might be in time then. Come on, Baumstein,' said Kirsten. As they went to leave the room, a couple of deputies burst in, holding guns at them, and they saw the FBI man's weapon. They almost started to shoot but Jim Baumstein put his hands up, let the weapon drop to the ground.

'Easy, fellas. Inside pocket, FBI. I'm the one that put the call through. Your sheriff's crooked.'

He saw the disbelieving faces.

'The call did come through from your office,' said the deputy, still pointing the weapon. He stepped forward and pulled out Jim's ID. 'Yes, he's good. Sorry,' said the deputy.

Jim bent down and picked up the weapon. 'It's not a problem. Any instructions from your sheriff, ignore them. I want you to secure this house. There are several men in the room over there. Make sure they don't leave, handcuff them. They're going down to the station. Outside, there's a load of Asian women stuck inside that van. They are trafficked girls. Get the appropriate services to them.'

'Where are you going, sir?' asked the deputy.

'Kyler's Peak. Any extra available units you've got aren't a part of your sheriff's people, send them.'

With that, Jim tore out of the room, Kirsten following him. She had done it. She had busted the trafficking ring. All she had to do now was complete the first job she'd been given and bring Melissa home.

Chapter 24

Kirsten could barely see Kyler's Peak as the car raced along the highway. There were a few other cars on the road and Jim received a call that his people were mobilising, but they were struggling to get through from Anchorage as the road to the south of the town of Kyler's Peak had become blocked. The good thing about this was that the articulated lorries with the girls on board were struggling to get out as well. Kirsten was more worried about Melissa up ahead, who had been her charge, the reason for coming, and she wasn't going to fail her now.

As the car got closer, she thought about the precipice that was Kyler's Peak, the large drop that gave the town its name. There was very little water now falling from the top; it had all been caked in ice, but the drop would kill anyone. It hadn't been that long ago when she was being forced that way, to be shot, and then dumped. And if it hadn't been for the man beside her, it was likely it would've ended up as her last trip.

As Jim continued to drive as fast as he could, he glanced over at Kirsten.

'You okay?'

'No,' she said, 'done your job, still got mine to do. I need to get that girl home.'

'Well, I've got plenty of stuff in the back that's going to help us,' he said. 'Clearly, you can handle yourself and clearly you might be outgunned this time. You're welcome to take any of the weapons from the rear.'

'Maybe,' said Kirsten, and realised they were approaching the peak. She told Jim to pull over a moment and asked for some binoculars. Both stepped out of the car while Jim fetched them from the boot, and she looked up at the peak.

'I can see a couple of them; the sheriff's there. I think he's got the girls with him, a load of other people as well.'

'How do we play this?' asked Jim. 'We can go up the road, but we're going to skid and slide like anything. By the time we get there if we haven't alerted them, they're going to have to be as deaf as anything. Despite the strength of this wind and snow, it won't mask our approach.'

'They're also going to come out shooting at you on the way down,' said Kirsten. 'Too easy for the girls to get caught in the crossfire.' She stared over at the precipice, looked at the drop. 'There's a path down the side of that, isn't there?' she said to Jim.

'I don't know,' he said, 'I'm not from here.'

'I've seen it, but it was all covered over, snowed in, but if I can get up that side, I can approach from a different angle. You could take their attention by coming up in the car on the road.'

'Do you want a gun?' he asked.

'No,' said Kirsten, 'I'm going to sneak up. My aim's to get the girls out of there so that you can open up with everything you've got.'

'How long is it going to take you to get up there?' Jim asked.

'Well, I don't see me getting up there any quicker than ten

minutes.'

'Ten minutes? If the path was clear, you'd struggle to get up there in ten minutes.'

'Ten minutes. You start up; you go at them. I'll be up there—just look out for me.'

Kirsten tore off her jacket, throwing it inside Jim's car. She felt an instant chill as her hair whipped around her blowing back into her eyes.

'For all you are a British agent, this is insane.'

'I'm not an agent,' said Kirsten; 'as for the other side of that statement, we'll find out.'

With that, she tore off, running through the snow, feeling the wind batter her, but heading to where she thought the path would start at the bottom of the precipice. She ran past the small pool at the bottom where they'd found the body of Peter Germaine. She didn't stop to look. However, she saw a piece of metal that was the top of the railing, there to protect you from falling off the path during your climb up the precipice. The path she thought weaved in and out, backwards and forwards, but the snow was already up and past the rail. She began up the path knowing there'd be no support, nothing to hold her in if she fell over.

Kirsten bent over, ran as hard as she could, pushing herself up the steep climb. The path twisted this way and that, and then moved inside of the drop with the trickling water falling down beyond her. It was as she got to this bit that she realised that the path was completely blocked. In front of her, there was a large overhang, but snow had fallen down the path blocking it up to the roof.

She would have to go up onto the rocks and climb across, but they were filled with ice, and picking her way through them was going to be difficult. Yet, she didn't have time to think about it. 'Ten minutes,' she'd said to Jim. If she was lucky, they had another seven left. She threw herself out, grabbing a hold of one of the rocks, and then swung her legs back and forward so she could rotate onto the next one. She put her hand up, felt it grip hard and tight, and then released her other hand to swing along again.

A tree branch got in her way, strewn across, and she reached up, pulling herself up with her left hand, then swung her right, grabbing hold of a rock, feeling it securely in her hand. She let go with the left hand to swing across and suddenly the right hand gave way. It wasn't the ice on the rock, the rock itself had given and Kirsten began to fall. She reached out with her left hand, grabbing wildly as the wind raged around her.

Suddenly she grabbed hold of the branch swinging backwards and forwards by one hand. She felt like her shoulder was going to rip out and try as she might, she was struggling to get her right hand up onto a branch as well. The branch began to swing. Kirsten desperately raised her legs up. Just as her hand gave way, she wrapped them around the branch.

It started to descend, and she swung herself back in towards the rock, catching hold with both hands as the branch suddenly gave away. She untwisted her legs, letting the branch drop, and found herself hanging once again underneath the precipice.

There was no time to spare, no time to think about what had been done, about whether the climb up now was sensible. She took a small handhold off to her left with one hand, and then, after securing that, made the climb with the next. It took her another two minutes to be able to swing back in onto the path. As she landed on it, Kirsten breathed deeply and then thought of up ahead. She couldn't get there before Jim; there was no way now.

The path came out again from cover, and she felt more exposed to the elements with the snow almost blinding her as she ran forward. The path twisted this way and that way and while, at times, it was incredibly steep and hard going, at least it was clear.

As Kirstin approached the top of the precipice, the path was off to one side, adjacent to where the river ended its passage and began to drop down the precipice. Carefully, she climbed up a little bit further and then stopped suddenly, seeing a blonde-haired girl walking forward, dressed in stockings and underwear. Kirsten knew the face immediately; that was Melissa, and across from her was another girl, this time fully clothed but with dark hair. It must have been the mayor's daughter.

'This will end it,' she heard the sheriff shouting over to some Italians.

'It better had. They're not impressed down south with how this has gone. If you don't clean this up, he will come for you.'

He'll come for you anyway, thought Kirsten. *There's no way they're going to let a mess like this go unchecked.* Kirsten saw the sheriff pointing a gun at Melissa and he walked forward, pushing it into her back. Several of the Italians had guns too and there was no way she could run over and get to Melissa, not before one of them would have tagged her. The sheriff pushed her with the gunpoint in the back of the shoulder blades, and Kirsten watched the girl get to the precipice.

'You see, this is the problem; you don't stick your nose in. I'd shoot you and let you fall but it's too kind for what you've done to me. You'll go over alive, you'll feel that every step of the way down. You're going to pay for what you've done.'

Kirsten watched as the pistol pushed into the girl's shoulder blades. Desperately, she tried to force against it, but she was slipping forward. A foot from the edge, Kirsten wondered should she make a move and was cursing Jim because he should have been here by now. He should be shooting.

Well, there was no point worrying about it, maybe he had trouble getting up the slope, maybe there was somebody further down that intercepted him. Kirsten could feel the sweat on her brow despite the fact she was cold. Her T-shirt was now soaked through, the black jeans as well, but she blew all that out of her mind to focus on what to do next.

She looked across the precipice towards the drop. If she ran from where she was and jumped, she could make it. She could land on the interior of the precipice. She wasn't sure how she'd get back out, but she could do it. Her eyes looked down at the distance she had climbed up. If she got it wrong, she was dead. She watched the girl slip forward, pushed by the point of the gun until suddenly, her feet began to slide and she tumbled forward.

Kirsten was on the move before the girl's feet had even left the snow. She ran hard, focusing only on the point she wanted to jump to. As she got close to the edge of the precipice, she let go, throwing her arms out in front of her. Melissa fell in front of her, and Kirsten hit her in the side as she jumped across. Together they both fell a good ten to twelve feet down before Kirsten's momentum carried her beyond Melissa and one foot touched down.

It slipped from under her, and Kirsten threw her left hand out to try and grab hold of anything. Her right hand slid down to Melissa. Kirsten felt the left hand slide once or twice and then she grabbed hold of something. It could be a root of a tree, but she wasn't sure. Her left hand slid down, went across the back of Melissa, who continued to descend until Kirsten caught her by the left hand. Suddenly the pair of them were left swinging.

Kirsten's shoulder pulled hard and she thought at first it had come out. Pain ran through her, screaming at her, but she hung on wishing that it would go away. Up above her, she heard gunfire, an automatic rifle whipping through the area. There were cries and shouts, a single gunfire back but Kirsten ignored it, pulling with her right hand, dragging Melissa up slowly but surely. She extended her legs to lift the girl as well who was struggling, shaking with fear.

'Get onto the ledge,' said Kirsten through gritted teeth. 'Get onto it. I can't hold you any longer.' Part of her thought she should just let go, she had done her work, but to let go was death.

'Give me a hand,' said Kirsten, 'give me a hand,' but the girl was on her back breathing heavily, shaking. Kirsten saw her backing away from the edge. *Hell*, she thought.

She needed to transfer her arms because she couldn't lift with her left one. She let her right hand swing, knew she was going to have to just . . . She swung it up once slowly, then a greater arc a second time, then a third time, but on the fourth time, she thrust her right arm as high as she could while letting her left arm go. One grip went, the other went, then her other hand reached up and curled around the same root.

Kirsten let out a sharp breath of relief, but she couldn't stop now. With her good shoulder, she started using her legs to scrabble up the side, pulling herself up and then rolling as best she could onto the ledge beyond. It took her a moment to catch her breath, to push herself back further until she hit rock beyond her. She sat upright in some sort of fashion, her shoulder in immense pain. Above her the gunfire continued.

'Cold,' said the girl in front of her.

'Come close, I can't move,' said Kirsten, 'wrap yourself to me.'

Together, the two of them hung on tight. Kirsten noticed that the gunfire above them had gone quiet. It would mean one or two things: either Jim had won and he would come to find them or the sheriff would, and he could pick them off easily trapped on this slope. She heard the crunch of footsteps on the far side moving to the path, she saw the long rifle and then the long black trousers up to a large coat and Jim's smiling face.

'Are you okay?' he asked.

'Can't move,' said Kirsten, 'you've got to go and get help. Get some people up to get us out of here.'

'I need a lot of people,' said Jim. 'Trust me, I need a lot of people. Stay close; try and stay warm.'

Kirsten nodded and her right arm pulled Melissa close to her. There wasn't a lot of heat, but they'd try and keep together, holding in that which they had.

Chapter 25

I t had taken over an hour to get someone on the scene, and Kirsten felt like the heat had been drained out of her body. The rescue team then had to set up a way of getting them out and pulling them back up the precipice. It took another hour before the pair of them were rushed into the back of an ambulance. Kirsten was taken to the hospital where she was kept in to warm her up and then they reset her shoulder, which had become dislocated.

She was glad when it was back in place, but it hurt like crazy. She eventually awoke in a hospital bed with Jim Baumstein's face at the far end of it. Kirsten tried to give a smile, but Baumstein held his hand up indicating she didn't have to and pulled a chair over close to her.

'You want a drink of some sort?'

'I don't think they do beer here, do they?' joked Kirsten.

'No,' laughed Jim. 'Although I thought you'd want something stronger than that. Here.' He reached over to a pitcher of water, poured some into a glass and held it up to her mouth.

'I can probably do that myself,' said Kirsten.

'Well, probably, but I'll do it for you. How's the arm?'

'Don't ask,' said Kirsten.

'You did good, though,' said Jim. 'You got her.'

'Not as good as you. What did you hit them with?'

'Might have had a sniper rifle at the car. I stopped a little bit short. Came all the way up and set up and was waiting for you to arrive. When she got to the precipice and suddenly she started to go and I saw you run, I opened fire, put most of them out. A couple got some shots back, but we got quite a few dead bodies up there. Couldn't risk only tagging them in case they got to you. The mountain rescue boys did a heck of a job pulling you out of that position. What made you jump for there?'

Kirsten laughed and then cursed as her shoulder went into spasm. 'I didn't really have that much of a choice,' she said. 'If I didn't land there, I was landing at the bottom. I'd already seen somebody at the bottom, and they weren't good.'

'Well,' said Jim, 'I've been in touch with my guys, and they've been in touch with your people.'

'I don't have people anymore.'

'That's what the boss said, but he also realises you've been very cooperative. You've also managed to not kill anyone, so everything's just been a bit of a scuffle. I've got a load of deputies wondering around shellshocked, unaware what their chief did.'

'Basically, it was the sheriff and the Italian mob trying to run human trafficking,' said Kirsten. 'and then we had a gold mine that was coming back into use.'

'That's right, and they were all going to set it up. Nice little investment, people coming up to the new mine, using up other mines around. The money would be coming in and the mayor would turn around after his initial disgust, or I have no doubt the sheriff would've done something else to him.

Orla Fontaine would've been making a packet over the top. Nice little arrangement until the Italians from down south got jealous of it. Oh, and your newspaper reporter stuck her nose in.'

'How is she?'

'Shook up. I'm not sure her stay was the most pleasant, but she's safe now. She had a touch of hypothermia, but she's got over that. She'll make a full recovery, thanks to you. It's going to take me a while to clean everything up.'

'Do we know who shot the deputy, though?'

'I do. Shot in an alleyway by Orla Fontaine. Apparently, the sheriff put her up to it. The idea was to frame you, but you got yourself out of there before anybody turned up. It caused the sheriff problems. Then he tried to frame you with the Italians. Shot the two of them in the hotel room. He was going to try and put a gun on you too, but apparently, you decided to run away when his guys took you up to the peak.

'He tell you all this?'

'Oh, yes. He's got a slight problem, you see. Large number of Italians looking for him. He wants to go into witness protection. He's singing like a bird, and we haven't promised him anything.'

'Well, I wish the very worst on him,' said Kirsten.

'That's about right,' said the American. 'But hey, you rest up. Don't worry about the bills. Look, we'll cover it. The least we can do for you, and we'll get you on a flight home. I'll need to do a couple of interviews with you. Go through what you did, when you did it, but we'll keep you out of the news. Can't have a limey coming over here and showing us our business.'

'Trust me, I'm not rushing back. I've seen enough of Kyler's Peak.'

'I don't blame you. I'll be glad to get back down to Anchorage and then head further south. It's kind of cold up here. I'm more used to LA, reasonable temperatures.' The man stood up and shook Kirsten's good hand. 'You get better. You hear? I'm going to be in touch.'

True to his word, John Baumstein took care of everything. Kirsten did have to settle down for a couple of interviews, but there was nothing taxing in that, and she was told she'd be flying home in a couple of days. She'd tried to call Craig, but no one would answer and so she spoke to Macleod asking him to drop in again. Macleod said he'd been keeping an eye, but there was nothing wrong with reminding him. The man had enough to do. That was sure.

When Kirsten stepped out of the hospital, she looked on a landscape that was covered in snow, but the sun was shining. The cool, crisp air felt good after having been in the hospital's stuffy confines for so long. The shoulder was recovering, but it would still need rest and she wasn't looking forward to the long flight home. She was chauffeured down to Anchorage by one of the deputies. They seemed to apologise every step of the way, and, on arrival, carried her bag in for her and assisted her with check-in before departing very apologetically. The woman at the desk handed her a ticket, which Kirsten saw was in business class when she picked up her phone to call Baumstein and thank him for it.

'I didn't do anything. I never upgraded you. I take care of a lot of things, but I'd have trouble pushing that one through. Besides, wouldn't want to see you arrive that way on the other side; it gets attention.'

Kirsten thanked him anyway and sat down in the departure lounge thinking of what was being said. When she'd come over, someone had followed her. Someone had almost tried to stop her arriving or had they? She'd been in the aircraft and then in the toilet cubicle at the back, and he'd come in after her. Maybe he was just going to give her a warning. Maybe. Who could tell? But she'd keep her eyes open.

Kirsten walked onto the plane and took a left turn up to the business class and then was advised that she was being upgraded further on. She looked at the host stewardess. She said it was perfectly okay, and she was led to a small private cubicle at the front. Inside was a first-class seat with a bed as well. Kirsten certainly wouldn't miss using it. However, she did wonder what was going on.

The aircraft took off, and they were soon up at the cruising height when a stewardess came in and asked if a gentleman could come in to see her. Kirsten nodded and then saw a face she tried to forget.

'Good evening, Miss Stewart. I take it the cabin's to your satisfaction. Still a little tight, though, but that's the thing about airplanes. You can't get the room on them.'

Kirsten looked up at Godfrey, head of the service she used to work for.

'If this is from you, I don't want it. You can take it and shove it.'

'After you had quietly sorted out our man on the way over, I thought on the way back I'd come and deliver the message personally. Better if the stewardess came in first, though. Make sure you didn't jump me.'

'Who's to say I won't now?'

'Well, your arm for one,' said Godfrey. 'Not in a good way, but our American friends have helped you back on the road to recovery, which is all good. I did wonder when you left the country what would become of you. Last time, things didn't go well.'

'Last time, we were fine. The two of us clear of you and just living our life. We would have been clear, except for what you caused.'

'It was unfortunate, but I couldn't have allowed her to live. Do you not see that? Might have caused her retaliation, but she was too dangerous. I did try to cover it up. Plane taking off and exploding. Maybe I should have had an explosion at the exchange, taken our guy out as well. That would have been more convincing. He was a worthwhile asset, though, not one I wanted to give up. Maybe I made that the wrong call.'

Kirsten shifted uneasily on the bed. 'What do you want from me?' she asked.

'I want an arrangement,' said Godfrey. 'You go all the way over here, not a single gunshot fired by you. Not a single person killed. I was worried when you came over. I thought she'll take the whole place out. You have a tendency to dispatch quite a number of people. I see in the end it was the FBI that took out most of them on the mountain. The sheriff killed people in your hotel room. Very good work. Clean in a lot of ways. You operated without any help whatsoever. Well almost. Cheeky Mr Chivers.'

'Why would I come back in? I'm not working under you again. I'll go and work in a bar if I have to, sweep the streets.'

'Oh, no. No, no,' said Godfrey, 'not back in the department. We have other things that need done, things we don't send the department on. Things that, if they go wrong, we can say wasn't us. Working on the quiet. The pay, of course, is considerably better. It's on a contract-by-contract basis and we get in touch when we need you. It could be home; it could be away. All your expenses will be covered, but you'll be on your own most of the time. You might have a few links to some people who can help but you seem to have a knack of bringing in the people you require. You even managed to bring in Mr Chivers last time when you were out in Zante.'

'I thought he worked for you,' said Kirsten.

'Mr Chivers is one of those people who I guess most of us don't know who he works for, self-serving in some ways and yet he has a conscience in there. Makes him dangerous in my line of work. Anna Hunt recommended you a long time ago to me. The thing is she was right. I just got where to put you wrong,' said Godfrey. 'If you want, you can be on my contact list. When a job comes up, you'll hear.'

Kirsten sat back on the bed, closed her eyes. She wanted the man to go away. She hated him. She saw Craig in his current state because of him, but it was true. What would she go on and do? This is what she was good at. She put her hand out and shook Godfrey's. 'I'd rather work alone than work for you. I'll name my price and I'll name what I will do and what I won't do, if you understand me?'

'Of course,' said Godfrey. 'Enjoy the flight. My cabin's just over if you want to reminisce.'

She saw the smile and thought it evil as he closed the door behind him. Kirsten pulled back the sheets of her bed. It was a small enough bed, but then again, they were in an aircraft. Kirsten thought about this and then she decided she would flick on the selection of movies that were available. She pressed the buzzer for the attendant.

'Bring me a beer,please,' she said, 'a couple of them, some food, something big and that will be me for the trip, thanks. Wake me up at least an hour before we land, if you can.'

The stewardess smiled and did so, and Kirsten sat for a couple of hours drinking her beer, eating the food, and then falling asleep. When she got into Heathrow, she was able to get a connection up to Inverness quickly and she placed a text call through to Macleod saying when she would be landing and asking for a lift. She didn't get a response before she got on the plane and realised she might have to take a taxi on arrival, but instead, when she exited from air side into the small baggage area at Inverness Airport, she saw Macleod standing.

He looked grim, but then again, he was rarely jolly. He walked over to her, saw the bag on one shoulder. 'You don't normally carry your bag on that side,' said Macleod, ever the detective. 'How did it go?'

'Rough. I popped the shoulder out at one point, but hey, I'm back. How's my man?'

Kirsten's heart sank because she saw Macleod's face drop.

'I went round this morning, tried to call him and didn't get an answer. When I got to your flat, I found him hanging from the ceiling. I think I was only a couple of minutes after he did it. I got him down, Kirsten. He's in hospital, but I got him down.'

She looked at Macleod and then flung one arm around him as she burst into tears.

'I got him,' said Macleod. 'I got him,' but all Kirsten could see was the horror of what happened to her partner and the fact that she'd just made a deal with the devil to go back into that sort of work.

Read on to discover the Patrick Smythe series!

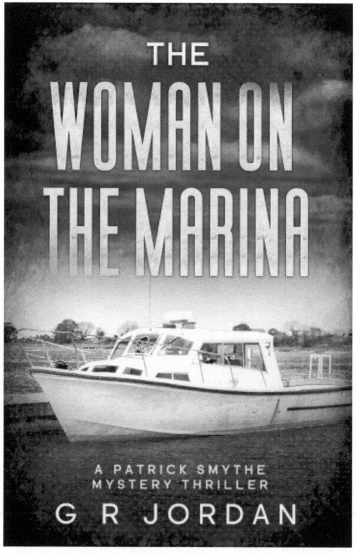

THE
WOMAN ON
THE MARINA

A PATRICK SMYTHE
MYSTERY THRILLER

G R JORDAN

Start your Patrick Smythe journey here!

Patrick Smythe is a former Northern Irish policeman who after suffering an amputation after a bomb blast, takes to the sea between the west coast of Scotland and his homeland to ply his trade as a private investigator. Join Paddy as he tries to work to his own ethics while knowing how to bend the rules he once enforced. Working from his beloved motorboat 'Craigantlet', Paddy decides to rescue a drug mule in this short story from the pen of G R Jordan.

Join G R Jordan's monthly newsletter about forthcoming releases and special writings for his tribe of avid readers and then receive your free Patrick Smythe short story.

Go to https://bit.ly/PatrickSmythe for your Patrick Smythe journey to start!

About the Author

GR Jordan is a self-published author who finally decided at forty that in order to have an enjoyable lifestyle, his creative beast within would have to be unleashed. His books mirror that conflict in life where acts of decency contend with self-promotion, goodness stares in horror at evil, and kindness blindsides us when we at our worst. Corrupting our world with his parade of wondrous and horrific characters, he highlights everyday tensions with fresh eyes whilst taking his methodical, intelligent mainstays on a roller-coaster ride of dilemmas, all the while suffering the banter of their provocative sidekicks.

A graduate of Loughborough University where he masqueraded as a chemical engineer but ultimately played American football, Gary had worked at changing the shape of cereal flakes and pulled a pallet truck for a living. Watching vegetables freeze at -40'C was another career highlight and he was also one of the Scottish Highlands "blind" air traffic controllers.

These days he has graduated to answering a telephone to people in trouble before telephoning other people to sort it out.

Having flirted with most places in the UK, he is now based in the Isle of Lewis in Scotland where his free time is spent between raising a young family with his wife, writing, figuring out how to work a loom and caring for a small flock of chickens. Luckily, his writing is influenced by his varied work and life experience as the chickens have not been the poetical inspiration he had hoped for!

You can connect with me on:

🌐 https://grjordan.com

📘 https://facebook.com/carpetlessleprechaun

Subscribe to my newsletter:

✉ https://bit.ly/PatrickSmythe

Also by G R Jordan

G R Jordan writes across multiple genres including crime, dark and action adventure fantasy, feel good fantasy, mystery thriller and horror fantasy. Below is a selection of his work. Whilst all books are available across online stores, signed copies are available at his personal shop.

Infiltrator! (A Kirsten Stewart Thriller #10)
Secrets being leaked from an overseas embassy. A mole too clever to be fooled by standard red herrings. Can Kirsten keep herself alive and find the mole before he discovers her cover?

Back in the pay of the British secret services, Kirsten must travel to South America where secrets are being passed through a mole known only as 'The Goldsmith'. But as Kirsten unearths the true nature of the information being passed, she finds herself in a race against time to stop a dirty bomb that goes right for the heart of British society.

The countdown has begun!

Dormie 5 (Highlands and Islands Detective Thrillers #25)
A clash of cultures at a golf club of distinction. The club secretary found sliced on the 15th tee box. Can Macleod and McGrath find the rogue player on the course before some else receives a two slash penalty?

With the building of the new parkland course beside Newton-moray's famous old links, tensions rise in the realms of the club's devoted golfers. But when there is talk of a professional tour event coming to the club and being switched to the new course, the gloves are off in a fight for the event. In the midst of the fervour, the club secretary is found dead over his golf trolley at the picturesque 15th hole. Can Seoras and Hope wade through the club politics and personalities to uncover a brutal killer, or will the clubhouse row lead to more patrons being teed up!

The match might be dormie, but they'll play to the death!

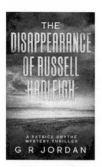

The Disappearance of Russell Hadleigh (Patrick Smythe Book 1)

https://grjordan.com/product/the-disappearance-of-russell-hadleigh

A retired judge fails to meet his golf partner. His wife calls for help while running a fantasy play ring. When Russians start co-opting into a fairly-traded clothing brand, can Paddy untangle the strands before the bodies start littering the golf course?

In his first full novel, Patrick Smythe, the single-armed former policeman, must infiltrate the golfing social scene to discover the fate of his client's husband. Assisted by a young starlet of the greens, Paddy tries to understand just who bears a grudge and who likes to play in the rough, culminating in a high stakes showdown where lives are hanging by the reaction of a moment. If you love pacey action, suspicious motives and devious characters, then Paddy Smythe operates amongst your kind of people.

Love is a matter of taste but money always demands more of its suitor.